A stranger lay next to her

Mia bolted upright in the bed and screamed.

The man sat up, too, causing the comforter to fall and reveal a snug gray T-shirt that outlined the impressive width of his shoulders. His gaze dropped to her breasts, which were visible through her pink nightshirt. A wickedly sexy smile kicked up one side of his mouth.

She grabbed the comforter, pulling it up to her neck, then jabbed the call button on the headboard several times.

The door to the suite swung open and Dr. Harlan Longo hurried into the room. "Is there a problem?"

She pointed to the intruder. "I just found this man in my bed!"

The man leaned against the headboard. "I don't think she was expecting me, Harlan."

"Nate Cafferty is part of the sleep experiment I'm conducting," the scientist explained. "*This* experiment tests the effects of sleeping with a stranger."

Mia looked over at Nate. Ruggedly handsome, he far surpassed any dream lover she'd ever imagined. And at that moment she half feared, and half hoped, she wouldn't be doing any sleeping at all....

Dear Reader,

I love to hear stories about how couples first met. What fascinates me is how one seemingly insignificant decision can change your life forever. Like when I chose to attend a college fraternity party instead of going home for the weekend. That's how I met my future husband. Or when a friend of mine decided to take a later airplane flight and found himself seated next to his future wife. Fate or coincidence?

When Mia Maldonado decides to take her friend's place in a sleep study, she has no idea that a sexy stranger named Nate Cafferty will be sleeping beside her. Fate or coincidence? You decide....

I love to hear from readers. You can reach me through my Web site at www.KristinGabriel.com or write to P.O. Box 5162, Grand Island, NE 68802-5162.

Enjoy!

Kristin Gabriel

Books by Kristin Gabriel

HARLEQUIN TEMPTATION

HARLEQUIN DUETS

KRISTIN GABRIEL

NIGHT AFTER NIGHT...

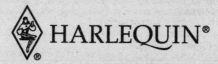

HARLEQUIN®

TORONTO • NEW YORK • LONDON
AMSTERDAM • PARIS • SYDNEY • HAMBURG
STOCKHOLM • ATHENS • TOKYO • MILAN • MADRID
PRAGUE • WARSAW • BUDAPEST • AUCKLAND

For Jean Louise

ISBN 0-373-69196-3

NIGHT AFTER NIGHT...

This edition published by arrangement with Harlequin Books S.A.

® and TM are trademarks of the publisher. Trademarks indicated with
® are registered in the United States Patent and Trademark Office, the
Canadian Trade Marks Office and in other countries.

www.eHarlequin.com

Printed in U.S.A.

1

MIA MALDONADO knew there was trouble the moment she heard "Blue Suede Shoes" blaring from the stereo speakers. Elvis always meant a crisis was brewing, so she proceeded warily through the front hall of the house, ready for anything.

The living room, which doubled as an office for her interior design business, was empty. Another bad sign. She'd leased the Tudor-style home a year ago, hoping the affluent Philadelphia neighborhood would bring wealthy, decorating-impaired clients to her door.

It had worked, too—until she'd started dating her design firm's best carpenter. She had a bad habit of falling too hard and too fast for men like Ian Brock. Men who looked so good in a pair of tight jeans that she overlooked their other genes—the ones that made them lie, cheat…and steal her sanity.

When she'd lived in Chicago, her heart had been broken so many times that she'd made a donation to the new cardiac wing at one of the city's hospitals in the name of all her mistakes. Mistakes like Bryan, Andrew, Jeff, Wyatt and Justin. Then she'd moved from Chicago to Philadelphia, ready for a fresh start.

But Ian was proof that she still hadn't learned her lesson. He'd dumped Mia three months ago, taking her heart and most of her clients along with him. Now she was determined that he'd be the last romantic mistake she ever made. From here on, Mia was going to follow her head instead of her hormones.

At least her best friend hadn't abandoned her yet. She'd met Carleen Wimmer a year ago, when they were the only two people at a matinee screening of *Gone With The Wind.* By intermission, they'd been sharing a large tub of buttered popcorn and commiserating over the fact that men like Clark Gable didn't exist anymore. By the end of the movie, Mia had offered Carleen a job as her office assistant.

Soon after, they decided to pool their limited resources by having Carleen move into the house. Kindred spirits, they shared a love of old movies, Thai cuisine and expeditions to flea markets. Carleen's gentle, cautious nature was the perfect complement to Mia's leap-before-you-look approach to life.

But Mia would lose her roommate next month when Carleen married Tobias Hamilton, a Philadelphia blue blood who could trace his family back to the *Mayflower.* He didn't seem to care that his fiancée had grown up in a trailer park instead of on Park Avenue.

Mia was happy for Carleen, even if Tobias was a little...bland. Maybe bland was good. Bland didn't run off with the first teenage bimbo to come along. Bland didn't break your heart. She was certainly in no position to criticize anyone else's love life. Not when her own had so recently ended in disaster.

She just hoped it wasn't contagious.

Mia turned down the sound on the stereo, then noticed the empty candy bar wrappers on the desk in the corner. Chocolate *and* Elvis. That meant it was serious. Carleen was on a strict diet so she could fit into the vintage wedding dress worn by all the Hamilton brides.

She shed her coat and purse, shoving her latest dating debacle to the back of her mind so she could tackle whatever awaited her. She found Carleen seated at the kitchen table, hunched over a carton of chocolate almond ice cream. Half of it was already gone.

"What's wrong?" Mia asked without preamble.

Carleen looked up at her, black mascara smudges beneath her green eyes. "I've ruined everything."

Mia grabbed a spoon from the drawer, then sat down across from her. "It can't be that bad."

"Oh, yes it can." Carleen dipped her spoon into the ice cream. "It's all over."

"What's all over?"

Carleen sucked in a shaky breath. "The wedding. Your business. My life."

Mia pulled the ice cream carton toward her, telling herself not to panic. "All right, let's start from the beginning. What happened?"

Carleen brushed back a wisp of blond hair stuck to her tear-stained cheek. "Toby left the country today. He's on an airplane right now, headed for Germany."

"Why?"

"Because his mother hates me." Her lower lip quivered. "She's only met me once, but she hates me all the same. Beatrice Hamilton thinks I'm not good enough to marry her only son."

"Hold on," Mia said. "Are you telling me his mother sent him off to Germany?"

Carleen shook her head. "No, but she's behind it. Toby has always been fascinated by show business. Recently, his mother arranged for him to meet a screenwriter at one of her fancy parties and now Toby's going to produce his movie. They're filming on location in Frankfurt for the next three weeks and he says he has to be there."

"But he'll be back in time for the wedding, won't he?"

"I hope so." Carleen pulled the ice cream carton back to her side of the table. "I'm telling you, Mia, that woman is determined to drive us apart. I tried to talk to Toby about it today when I took him to the airport, but we just got into a huge fight. He wouldn't even listen to me. He's more upset about Harlan than his mother."

"Whoa, back up a step," Mia said. "Who's Harlan?"

She heaved a long sigh. "I should have mentioned him first. Harlan Longo. You know, that millionaire who likes to play scientist?"

"Yes," Mia replied, more confused than ever, "what about him?"

"Well, I signed up for his three-week sleep study to save Mia's Makeovers. He's offering a three-thousand-dollar stipend to his research subjects and you mentioned just the other day that we needed to find money to advertise or the business is doomed."

Mia blinked at her. "You signed up to help me?"

Carleen's face softened. "It was the least I could do. I'll never be able to repay you for everything you've done for me. Giving me a job. Taking me in when I didn't have anywhere else to go. Treating me like a member of your family." A smile trembled on her lips. "You're the sister I never had."

Mia swallowed the huge lump in her throat, then chased it down with a spoonful of ice cream. "We're friends, Carleen. You don't owe me anything."

"Then think of it as my going-away present," Carleen replied. "Toby is talking about moving to California after we're married. He wants to live in Hollywood. I couldn't be happy knowing I left you behind with all those unpaid bills piling up. I had to do something."

At that moment, Mia realized just how much she was going to miss living with Carleen. "Don't worry about me. I'll be fine."

"Look, we've both been trying to ignore that business hasn't been too good around here lately. I've been using more and more red ink when I do the books. So when I received one of Harlan Longo's invitations to participate in his latest study, I thought it was the answer to all our problems."

"Harlan Longo's not even a real scientist, is he?"

"No, but he's really rich." Carleen licked the back of her spoon. "Rich enough that people call him eccentric instead of crazy. So if he wants to spend his money conducting sleep experiments, he can. I heard he even has some kind of fancy laboratory set up at his estate. That's where I'm supposed to go tonight. But…"

"But," Mia prodded.

Carleen sighed. "But Toby thinks Harlan Longo is unstable and doesn't want me to do it. He was *so* upset about it. The problem is that I've already used the stipend Harlan's paying to buy advertising time for Mia's Makeovers on the radio." She met Mia's gaze. "I wanted it to be a surprise."

"Oh, Carleen," Mia replied, realizing no one had ever done anything so unselfish for her before.

She'd grown up with parents who had taught her the value of hard work but who didn't understand her desire to build her own business. Though they had never said it aloud, she knew her family back in Chicago expected her to fail. An expectation that now seemed alarmingly possible.

Mia did believe advertising could save her business, but not at the expense of Carleen's relationship with Toby. "If Toby is that upset about it, then maybe you shouldn't do it."

"But the money…"

"I'll find a way to fix it," Mia told her, though she knew she'd never qualify for another loan.

"Ian Brock is the one who should fix it," Carleen sputtered. "He stole all your clients when he went to work for that big design company."

Mia shook her head. "I should have known better than to date a man who works for me. Especially when he happens to be one of the best carpenters in Philadelphia."

"That man can do amazing things with his hands," Carleen acknowledged.

"Believe me, I know." Memories flooded her and Mia's throat contracted. "But I have to quit dwelling on him and concentrate on finding new clients. I literally can't afford to let my personal life interfere with my business anymore. And you can't afford to put my business ahead of Toby."

Tears gleamed in her eyes. "I just don't know what I'll do if I lose him."

"You're not going to lose him," Mia assured her. Then a solution hit her that was so obvious she wondered why she hadn't thought of it sooner. "Why don't I just take your place tonight?"

Carleen blinked. "What?"

"I'll participate in the sleep study instead of you. It's not like I have a life right now anyway. Besides, that only seems fair since you're using the money to save my business."

"But Harlan Longo is expecting *me* to show up tonight," Carleen said. "I've already filled out a personality profile and signed a contract and everything. Who knows what he'll do if I bail out at the last minute?"

"I doubt he'll care," Mia replied. "These research projects are just a form of entertainment for him. No one takes them seriously."

"I'm not so sure," Carleen told her. "I think he takes them *very* seriously. At least, that's the impression I got when I talked to him on the telephone last week."

"Then I'll just pretend I'm you," Mia improvised, determined to find a way to make it work. "He'll never know the difference."

Hope mingled with uncertainty in Carleen's eyes. "I can't ask you to do that."

"You're not asking me," Mia replied, warming to the idea. "I'm volunteering. You didn't send him a picture of yourself, did you? I mean, I'm an Italian brunette and you're a blonde. He'd notice the difference right away."

"I didn't send him my picture." Carleen thought for a moment. "In fact, he didn't ask for any kind of physical description. Most of the questions on the profile were about my sleeping habits. What time I usually go to bed at night and how long I usually sleep—things like that."

"You'll have to brief me on all your answers before I leave tonight—" Mia reached over to close the lid on the ice cream carton "—just in case he asks me something about it."

"Do you really think we can get away with it?"

"Absolutely." Anticipation shot through Mia. Impersonating her best friend might be the perfect distraction she needed to get her mind off of Ian. "All I have to do is sleep there, right?"

"Right," Carleen confirmed. "From what I understand, Harlan wants to study the effects of different environments on sleep patterns. An example he gave me is sleeping in a hot room compared to a cold one, or with all the lights turned on instead of off."

"That sounds simple enough."

"You're supposed to pack your favorite pajamas," Carleen advised her, "and bring your own pillow. Harlan made it very clear that he wants his research subjects to be as comfortable as possible."

"Is that all I need to do?"

Carleen shrugged. "As far as I know. The contract was full of a lot of legal mumbo jumbo, so I just skimmed most of it. I'm sure he'll explain everything in more detail when you get there."

Mia glanced at her watch. "Then I'd better go upstairs and start packing."

Carleen rose from her chair. "I can't wait to call Toby and make up with him. Are you sure you don't mind standing in for me? Or rather, sleeping in for me?"

Mia smiled. "Just call me Carleen."

"This Carleen Wimmer is trouble." Nate Cafferty handed the file folder to his client, then leaned back in his chair.

"I knew it." Beatrice Hamilton scanned the slim contents. She was in her midfifties and reeked of old money. Her perfectly manicured hands sorted through the papers in the file, her aquiline nose wrinkling in disdain.

"My son has always had horrendous taste in women," she said at last, "but they were all just harmless flings. He never considered actually marrying one of them before."

"Then the engagement is still on?"

"I'm afraid so." She looked hopefully at him. "Unless you have something that will convince Tobias to dump her. That is why I hired you, Mr. Cafferty."

He chafed at her haughty tone. Beatrice Hamilton fit the stereotype of interfering mother to a tee. The fact that she was rich only gave her more resources to meddle. Like hiring a private investigator to dig up dirt on her son's fiancée.

Nate usually tried to avoid this kind of family squabble, but Mrs. Hamilton was paying him enough to make it worth his while. Besides, the case intrigued him.

"Well?" Mrs. Hamilton prodded. "What exactly do you have on her?"

"Nothing substantial," he answered. "Yet."

Her mouth thinned. "But you just said she was trouble."

"I think she is," he replied. "The woman didn't even exist until a year ago. At least, no woman by the name of Carleen Wimmer existed. Your son's fiancée created a whole new identity for herself."

Satisfaction gleamed in the older woman's pale blue eyes. "So I was right about her. She is some kind of scam artist. I suspected as much when I met with her."

"When was this?"

"A few weeks ago, when I realized that Tobias was truly serious about going through with this ridiculous marriage. I called her and asked her to meet me at the Carlisle Hotel. I'd never allow a woman like that into my home."

Or a man like me, Nate thought to himself. No doubt she could spot his lack of breeding a mile away. He'd been born to a single mother with a drinking problem, so had grown up on the mean streets of Philadelphia fighting for survival. He'd made it, thanks to Harlan Longo, though he still carried the scars—both inside and out. Mrs. Hamilton didn't ask about his background and probably didn't care as long as she got what she wanted.

"And the tart had the audacity to turn down the generous offer I made to convince her to disappear from my son's life."

Good for her, Nate thought to himself.

Mrs. Hamilton sniffed. "That's when I knew I needed to find something to use against her, so I hired you."

Nate wished she'd hired him sooner. The wedding deadline was fast approaching and he would have liked more time to investigate the woman before he initiated contact. He didn't even have a picture of Carleen Wimmer yet, though he wouldn't need one after tonight. "Does your son know I'm investigating his fiancée?"

"Of course not. He'd be livid if he knew." She rose to her feet, obviously too agitated to stay seated any longer. "But someone has to look out for his interests. With his father gone, that responsibility falls to me."

Nate pulled another file folder from his desk and opened it. "According to my research, Tobias turned twenty-eight last March. Don't you think he's old enough to be responsible for himself?"

"What is this?" She snatched the folder out of his hands. "Who gave you permission to snoop around my son's life, Mr. Cafferty?"

"I don't need permission," he replied evenly. "When I take on a case, I have to know all the facts—including facts about your son. If you don't like it, you can hire another investigator."

Color flooded Mrs. Hamilton's patrician face. No doubt she wasn't used to anyone, especially an employee, standing up to her.

"Perhaps I will." She set the folder back on Nate's desk. "It all depends on how you plan to get rid of this woman and how long it's going to take. The wedding is less than a month away."

"It's not my job to get rid of her." Nate wanted to make that clear. "I'm simply gathering information about her. How you choose to use that information is up to you."

"I'll use it to save my son," she replied, squaring her shoulders, "any way that I can."

Nate wondered if Tobias Hamilton chose his women on the basis of how much they'd irritate his mother. He'd never met the man, but so far he wasn't impressed. His limited investigation had turned up a spoiled rich boy with too much time and too much money on his hands. At the moment, he was in Germany playing movie producer and leaving his fiancée behind to the wolves.

The fact that Nate was one of those wolves didn't bother him. If Carleen Wimmer had nothing to hide, then she had nothing to fear from him. He'd do his job, but he wouldn't try to destroy her. That was Mrs. Hamilton's job. Or more precisely, her pleasure.

"So what happens next?" his client asked, obviously eager to begin the demolition.

"I've set up a way to meet her through an old friend of mine," Nate explained. "His name is Harlan Longo and he was happy to offer his assistance."

"The name sounds familiar." Her brow furrowed. "Isn't he that scientist who tried to prove that sleeping on feather pillows increased fertility rates or some such nonsense? I remember reading about it in the newspaper."

Nate smiled. "He's the one."

"Quite the eccentric," she said. "Are you certain he can be trusted?"

"Yes." Nate didn't elaborate. He wasn't going to justify his actions to this woman. She either trusted him to do his job or not. "I asked him to send Carleen Wimmer an invitation to participate as a research subject in his latest sleep study—with a generous stipend, of course."

"I assume she accepted," Mrs. Hamilton said dryly, "since she's certainly not averse to sleeping for money."

"She did," Nate acknowledged. "Harlan gave me full access to the personality profile she filled out—though I have no way of knowing how much of it is true. But I'll be meeting her tonight in Harlan's laboratory."

"Won't that make her suspicious?"

"Not if I'm just another one of his guinea pigs. I'll find some way to introduce myself and get to know her." Nate rose to his feet, ready to end the interview. "Then you'll have the answers to all your questions about her."

She stared at him for a long moment. "You're a very confident young man, aren't you?"

"I know how to do my job."

"Quite handsome, as well," she continued, looking him up and down, "in a rough sort of way. And you have the presence and athletic physique that many young women seem to find appealing these days. Perhaps you are the right man for this job after all."

Nate walked over to open the office door for her. "I'll send you an update in a few days."

"Sooner, if possible, Mr. Cafferty." She picked up her purse. "I don't like to be kept waiting."

Nate watched her walk daintily to the black Lincoln Town Car parked in front of his office. She might look the part of the refined lady, but beneath that austere exterior was a woman not afraid to get dirty.

Now it was up to him to find the dirt.

2

MIA HALF EXPECTED to find something out of Frankenstein's laboratory when she went in search of the Longo Research Center later that evening. She held her overnight bag in one hand and a map of the estate grounds in the other. The map had been given to her by the guard at the front gate, right after he'd taken her car keys.

Walking almost half a mile in the crisp autumn air gave her plenty of time for second thoughts about impersonating Carleen. She'd read about Harlan Longo's eccentricities in the newspaper, which were often accompanied by stories about his generosity to various charities. But traversing his estate by foot in the waning twilight gave her a disturbing glimpse of the man throwing this slumber party.

He'd built a moat around his sprawling mansion, along with a rustic suspension bridge leading to the research center. A rowboat peopled with two rubber blow-up dolls floated on the stagnant water. One of the dolls even held a fishing pole. Chickens roamed freely on the grounds and roosted in an old yellow school bus that still had the words Paddington Middle School printed on the side.

By the time she reached the solid steel door of the Longo Research Center, she had no doubt old Harlan was crazy. Now she was beginning to wonder about her own sanity for volunteering to sleep in this madhouse every night for the next three weeks.

A rusty horseshoe hung on the door, right under the words LONGO RESEARCH CENTER spelled out in bright red letters. After searching in vain for a doorbell, she lifted the horseshoe and rapped it three times against the door. When she heard the heavy footsteps on the other side, she braced herself for a humpbacked Igor to greet her.

But the man who opened the door stood straight and tall, a mane of smooth white hair brushing the shoulders of his white lab coat. "Greetings!"

"I'm...Carleen Wimmer," she said, slightly unnerved by the two security cameras trained on her. "Mr. Longo is expecting me."

The man grinned. "Indeed, I am! Please come in, Carleen Wimmer. Welcome to my laboratory."

She stepped through the door, surprised to find it actually looked like a laboratory on the inside. The sleek, modern decor impressed her. Black and white ceramic tiles formed a wheel shape on the floor, leading to a center hub that contained a round stainless steel desk that was the focal point of the large room. Each one of the tile spokes of the wheel led to a door, about twelve in all, which she assumed were entrances to the individual sleeping suites.

The doors were all closed and the hub, filled with gleaming chrome fixtures, was curiously empty of people. Uneasiness filled her. "Am I the only one here?"

"So far," Harlan replied. "I staggered the appointed arrival times so I could meet with each of my research subjects individually."

She glanced at her watch. "I hope I'm not late."

"You're right on time," he assured her, taking the overnight bag out of her hand. "Did you bring a pillow?"

"It's in my bag."

"Very good." He reached out to pluck a small feather off the sleeve of her jacket. "I'm sorry about the long walk. Cars scare my chickens," he said over his shoulder as he led her to one of the closed doors.

"That's all right," she said, following him. "All that fresh air will probably help me sleep better."

He opened the door to the suite, an excited twinkle in his eye. "I hope you like what I've done with the room."

The first thing she noticed was the jukebox. It stood in the far corner, close to the queen-sized bed. The soft strains of "Are You Lonesome Tonight?" filled the air. The song went well with the framed head shot of Elvis above the headboard and the gold lamé comforter that was embroidered with tiny guitars and musical notes. But she found the floor-to-ceiling mural of Graceland covering one wall to be the most impressive part of the room.

"Well?" Harlan asked, visibly proud of his decorating efforts. "What do you think?"

"I'm speechless," she answered honestly.

Carleen had told her that she'd listed Elvis songs as her "comfort music" on the personality profile. Harlan had obviously taken that little tidbit and run with it.

"Look at this," he said, leading her over to the jukebox. "It doubles as a biomonitor to record your vital signs. It even has retractable cables to hook you up to the machine."

He pulled one out, demonstrating how the lead reached the bed. Then he let it go and it sprang back into the jukebox with a loud pop.

"Wow," she said, wondering what other surprises awaited her.

He walked over to the bed and pressed a button on the headboard. "Feel free to ring anytime you need assistance. Myself or one of my assistants will be right outside in the control center. This facility is completely secure. The door to your suite automatically locks."

That thought made her a little uneasy. "So I'll be locked in?"

"Not at all," he assured her. "If you wish to exit the room, all you have to do is press the button next to the door. That signals one of my assistants to press the corresponding button on the control panel and the door will unlock."

"Got it," Mia replied.

"You'll be perfectly safe here," he assured her. "You probably noticed the security cameras when you entered the lab. I have cameras positioned around the entire estate. No one can enter my property without my knowledge."

A knock sounded on the door, then a petite young Asian woman wearing a pink polka-dot lab coat entered the room. "Did you need something, Dr. Longo?"

"Yes, Hannah, I'd like to introduce you to Carleen Wimmer. She'll be sleeping in the Elvis suite for the next three weeks."

"Nice to meet you, Ms. Wimmer," Hannah said, holding out her hand.

Mia shook it, surprised by her firm grip. "Please call me Carleen."

"If you wish."

Longo set Mia's bag on the end of the bed. "Hannah is assigned to work this half of the sleep lab. She'll get you all hooked up for tonight, then I'll be in to answer any questions you might have and to tuck you in."

"All right," Mia said with a smile. No one had tucked her into bed since she was ten years old—not that her Italian mother hadn't tried. But Mia's independent streak had kicked in at an early age.

She still remembered the time she'd informed her grandmother that she never intended to marry because husbands were too bossy, though she did plan to have six children. The poor woman had almost keeled over from that pronouncement.

Shocking her family had turned into a fairly routine occurrence, though she rarely did it intentionally. They just didn't understand that she wanted more than the life they had mapped out for her.

Like taking karate lessons instead of ballet. Or skipping out on catechism class so she could rehearse with her heavy metal band. Her cousins had lovingly dubbed her the black sheep of the family, though Mia hardly deserved the title. She wasn't rebellious, just unconventional by Maldonado standards.

When her parents had balked at her decision to enroll in design school instead of choosing a more traditional career like teaching or nursing, Mia had chosen to pay her own way through college.

Then she'd moved to Philadelphia, choosing the city by spreading a map of the United States in front of her, closing her eyes and letting fate guide her finger. When she'd first arrived, Mia had found a job designing display cases for a furniture outlet store until she'd saved enough money to strike out on her own.

Judging by her current financial predicament, she hadn't saved enough. But the last thing she wanted to do was return to Chicago a failure, fulfilling her family's dire predictions. Mia wanted to prove to them and to herself that she could make it on her own.

If the radio advertisements brought in enough new clients, Mia's Makeovers could survive. Her only obstacles were succeeding in impersonating her best friend and sleeping in an Elvis suite.

At least she'd passed the first test. Harlan left the suite without a backward glance, apparently convinced that she really was Carleen Wimmer.

"You can change in Graceland," Hannah said as she fiddled with the dials on the jukebox.

Mia's gaze went to the elaborate mural on the wall. "I don't understand."

"There's a pocket door that slides open," she replied, pointing to the door of the mansion. "It leads to a small bathroom."

Mia didn't see the door until she walked right up to it. "This is amazing," she said, sliding it open.

"Dr. Longo spares no expense to make his research

subjects comfortable," Hannah replied, fluffing the pillow before laying it on the bed.

"Is he really a doctor?" Mia asked.

"He's made some very generous endowments to Parker University, so they gave him an honorary degree. He even set up an internship program for students interested in research and development. That's how I came to be here." A smile flitted across her small mouth. "Though I have to admit it's not quite what I expected."

"Me, either," Mia acknowledged, grabbing her overnight bag off the bed. By the time she emerged from the Graceland bathroom, Hannah was ready to hook her up to the jukebox.

She climbed awkwardly into the bed as Elvis sang "It's Now or Never."

"So is this your first time as a research subject?" Hannah asked, sweeping the bangs off Mia's forehead to attach the wire cables.

"Yes," she replied, then hoped that was the right answer. Carleen hadn't been able to remember all of the questions on the personality profile.

Mia took a deep breath, telling herself not to panic. What was the worst that Dr. Longo could do if he discovered she wasn't Carleen? *Kick her out of his sleep lab and demand his money back.*

Okay, the money would be a problem. But worrying about it wouldn't help. She'd done enough worrying while dating Ian. His erratic behavior the last few weeks of their relationship had turned her into someone she hadn't recognized—a needy, insecure woman. She had spent hours analyzing and reanalyzing everything he said and did when she should have just trusted her instincts and dumped the cheating jerk before he dumped her.

Now she had a chance to start over. Pretending to be Carleen would give her an opportunity to break out of all her bad habits. To create a new and improved Mia Maldonado.

"Carleen?"

She blinked, then realized Hannah had just asked her another question. "I'm sorry, what did you say?"

She smiled. "You're all set now. Can I get you anything?"

"No, I'm fine." Mia folded her arms on top of the thick comforter, her fingers nervously strumming the embroidered guitar threads.

"Dr. Longo will be in soon."

"All right." She kept her gaze on the ceiling, afraid if she moved one of the electrodes would become disconnected. Hannah disappeared from view and she heard the door creak open, then close again as the assistant took her leave.

A moment later, the door creaked open again and Harlan Longo walked into her view.

"Hannah tells me you're ready to go to sleep."

"I'll do my best," she replied, not feeling the least bit sleepy.

"I know you will." He reached out to pat her shoulder gently. "And I'd like to thank you for assisting me in my research."

"What exactly are you testing in this room?" she asked, wondering if she'd wake up in subzero temperatures. "If I remember right, you're researching how different environments affect sleep patterns."

"That's correct," he replied. "But we never tell our research subjects what to expect ahead of time. That way, your anticipation of the change in environment won't affect the readings. For instance, a subject anticipating a hot room might throw off the bed covers before he goes to sleep. If it's a cold room, he might wear his socks to bed."

Mia thought the anticipation of not knowing what was going to happen might have a greater affect on the readings, but it was Dr. Longo's experiment so she didn't question him on it.

"Don't worry," he said, sensing her apprehension. "The music will help you fall asleep."

She considered telling him it would do just the opposite, but didn't have the heart after he'd gone to so much trouble with the Elvis room. The more time she spent with Harlan, the more she liked the man—even if he was a little odd.

He walked over to the door and dimmed the lights. "Sweet dreams, Carleen."

She smiled to herself in the soft glow of the jukebox, thinking Harlan would make a better grandfather than scientist. "Good night."

As he left the room, she wondered if the rumors she'd heard about him were true. After his wife's death, there had been subtle speculation in the newspapers that his neglect of her medical condition had led to her early demise, despite the Longos having enough money to afford the best medical care in the world.

Now, having met the man, she simply couldn't

believe it. Harlan didn't seem like a ruthless businessman to her. He might be a little strange, judging by his various research projects, but so were a lot of people.

She lay stiffly in the bed, too aware of the wire cables tethering her to the jukebox to relax. Several minutes passed, until she finally grew bored enough to close her eyes and practice the relaxation techniques that Carleen had taught her after her breakup with Ian.

Breathing in deeply through her diaphragm, she held her breath for a moment, then slowly released it, letting the tension flow out of every pore of her body. She repeated this technique several more times, gradually becoming more comfortable.

When Elvis began to sing "Love Me Tender," the music soothed her like a lullaby. By the end of the song, she forgot about the relaxation breathing and began to drift off to sleep.

Floating in a twilight haze, she was dimly aware of the door creaking open, then closing again. Footsteps padded on the carpet, but she kept her eyes closed, drowsily telling herself it was just Hannah coming to check on her.

Mia dozed, barely aware of someone moving quietly around in the room. Then her senses came alive at the sound of the bedsprings bouncing beside her and the spicy scent of male aftershave.

She opened her eyes and the glow of the jukebox revealed a man lying next to her in bed, staring right back at her.

Ruggedly handsome, with a slight crook in his

nose and a small scar over his right eyebrow, he far surpassed any dream lover she'd ever imagined. But when he spoke, Mia knew she wasn't dreaming.

"So what's a nice girl like you doing in a place like this?"

She bolted upright in the bed and screamed.

He sat up, too, the gold lamé comforter falling to reveal a snug gray T-shirt that outlined the impressive width of his shoulders and the rippling muscles of his chest and torso. He wore his hair short, like a Marine, but she couldn't tell the color of his eyes because his gaze had dropped to her breasts, where her pert nipples were visible through the thin cotton fabric of her pink nightshirt.

She grabbed the comforter, pulling it up to her neck, then jabbed the button on the headboard several times. "What do you think you're doing in here?"

A wickedly sexy smile kicked up one side of his mouth. "I think I just asked you that same question."

Before she could reply, the door to the suite swung open and Harlan hurried into the room. "Is there a problem?"

She pointed to the intruder. "I just found this man in my bed!"

"So?" Harlan replied, looking perplexed.

She blinked. "So? That's all you have to say? *So?*"

The man leaned back against the headboard. "I don't think she was expecting me, Harlan."

That was the understatement of the century. She turned to Harlan, the wire cables limiting her movement. "I don't know what kind of girl you think I am, but if this research center is just a front for making a porn movie or is some kind of kinky sex club, then I'm not interested—"

"Now just hold on there," Harlan admonished, raising both hands. "This is legitimate scientific research, Carleen. You're going to skew all the readings if you keep jumping around like that."

"Then do something about him," she insisted, forcing herself to lie still. "Call the police or one of your security guards and get him out of here."

Harlan's brow furrowed as he moved around to her side of the bed. "I don't think you understand, Carleen. Nate Cafferty is your new environment."

She blinked. "What?"

"This is an experiment about how different environments affect sleep patterns," he reminded her, "as well as how quickly we adapt to them."

"I don't want to adapt to him," she replied, needing to make that very clear. "I don't even *know* him."

"That's the point, my dear," Harlan said, as if it all made perfect sense. "The specific environment I designed for you is *sleeping with a stranger.* That's why we waited until you fell asleep so we could establish your baseline readings before we let Nate join you in bed."

"You can't be serious." She glanced at Nate, who seemed to enjoy watching her come unraveled. "I can't sleep with him. I...I'm engaged."

"Yes, I know, but I still don't understand why you're so upset." Harlan's brow crinkled. "All the possibilities were spelled out in the contract."

She swallowed a groan. Apparently, Carleen had missed that little detail when she'd skimmed over the legal mumbo jumbo. "I'm upset because no woman in her right mind would put herself in a situation like this."

"You have nothing to fear from Nate," Harlan assured her. "He won't hurt you."

She looked between the two men. "So you really expect me to go through with this?"

"That's completely up to you," Harlan replied. "I never force my research subjects to do anything they don't want to do. But I have to admit I'll be very disappointed if you decide to return the money and quit the sleep study."

She hesitated. Returning the money wasn't an option. But how could she spend the next three weeks in bed with a stranger? She turned to Nate, hoping he'd at least act the gentleman and withdraw.

But the man lying beside her didn't say a word. He just gazed back at her with eyes that she could now see were the same shade of verdant green as the leaves of the stately pin oak trees painted on the Graceland mural.

A keen intelligence shone from those eyes. And something else. Something that made her want to squirm beneath the covers. Mia wondered if she really could trust Nate. She wasn't the best judge of a man's character. Ian Brock was proof of that. But what choice did she have at this point?

"I suppose we could try it," she said, surrendering to the inevitable, "at least for tonight."

"Wonderful," Harlan exclaimed, stepping up to the jukebox. "Now let me check to make sure all of these connections are still secure."

"Why doesn't Nate have to wear them?" she

asked, knowing she probably resembled Medusa with all the cables sticking out of her head. The fact that she had washed off her makeup didn't improve her mood, either.

At least Nate didn't seem to mind her appearance. He settled back onto his pillow as Harlan tucked the covers around her.

"Nate's vital signs aren't relevant to my research," Harlan told her. "For this particular study, I'm only interested in how your sleep patterns are affected at different phases of the relationship."

"But we don't have a relationship," Mia reminded him. "We haven't even met before tonight."

Harlan grinned. "That's why this study fascinates me so much. Because when you sleep with someone every night, even platonically, you have to develop some kind of relationship—good or bad."

She glanced at Nate, wondering if this was some kind of test of her willpower. Having recently sworn off bad boys, she now found herself in bed with one. Only he far surpassed the Justins, Andrews and Ians of her past. Her awareness of him pulsed through every cell in her body, making her hot and cold at the same time.

Not a good sign.

Mia forced herself to look away and took a deep breath. If she could resist him, she could resist anyone. The key was to avoid him as much as possible while sharing the same bed. That meant not looking at him, not talking to him, and *definitely* not touching him.

Harlan lowered the volume on the jukebox. "Now

let's try this again, shall we?" He walked to the door, his hand resting on the night switch. "Goodnight, Carleen. Goodnight, Nate."

Then he left them alone in the dark, the only sound in the room Elvis crooning a song that seemed appropriate for the occasion.

"All Shook Up."

3

NATE HAD Carleen Wimmer exactly where he wanted her.

Now he just had to figure out a way to make her talk. Not that he had much in common with Elvis aficionados—even if this one had breathtaking brown eyes and a killer body that had *him* all shook up.

No wonder Tobias Hamilton wanted to marry her.

Nate couldn't understand how anyone could find a trip to Germany more appealing than the woman beside him. Voluptuous didn't begin to describe her. He'd climbed into bed with plenty of women, but the sight of her, asleep and unaware, had caught him like a sucker punch to the gut the moment he'd lain down beside her.

The silky waves of thick brown hair tousled on the white pillow. The way her wide pink mouth parted slightly, begging to be kissed. The generous cleavage that almost spilled out of the thin cotton nightshirt she wore. If he was her fiancé, he'd never leave her side or her bed.

But he wasn't her fiancé. Not even close. He was her worst nightmare—if she had something to hide. That's what he was here to find out, Nate reminded himself. And he couldn't let a pair of big brown eyes—or a pair of erect nipples—distract him from that mission.

"You never answered my question," he said, breaking the heavy silence between them.

She lay with her back to him, but he could tell by her stiff posture and erratic breathing that she was still wide awake.

"What question?"

He liked the husky depth of her voice. It brought to mind vintage movie starlets like Katherine Hepburn and Lauren Bacall. Strong, independent women who knew how to drive a man to distraction. "How a nice girl like you ended up in a sleep study like this."

She rolled over to face him, her expression hidden in the shadows. "It's a long story."

"We've got all night."

She hesitated, and for a moment he thought she was going to turn her back and ignore him. Instead, she slid her slender hands under her pillow, pulling it down in front of her like a protective shield. "I guess you could say I'm doing it for the money."

"Me, too," he acknowledged, though he didn't tell her who was paying him. "So that gives us at least one thing in common."

"Poverty?"

He chuckled. Not only beautiful, but witty. A lethal combination. "Okay, make that two things. I was talking about finding creative ways to make money."

As he waited for her response, Nate knew it was too much to hope that she'd confess her upcoming marriage to Tobias Hamilton was her latest money-making scheme.

"I'm trying to save my business."

Now he knew she was lying. He'd gotten access to Carleen Wimmer's credit reports just this afternoon and there was no way she'd ever qualify for any kind of business loan. "You own a business?"

She cleared her throat. "Actually, it belongs to a good friend of mine, Mia Maldonado. I'm the office assistant for Mia's Makeovers, a design business she runs out of the house we both live in. I guess that's why I feel like the business belongs to me, too."

Her explanation didn't quite ring true, though if he stared into those eyes long enough, he'd believe any word out of her lovely mouth. Her eyes looked even sexier in the glow of the jukebox and he wondered how many men had lost themselves in their warm chocolate depths.

Nate hated to admit that Mrs. Hamilton might be right about her son's fiancée. She was a femme fatale, with an aura of wanton innocence that few men could resist. The kind of woman who could easily make a weak man surrender his heart as well as his money to her without a struggle.

Nate had only known Carleen for a few minutes and he was already mesmerized. But he wasn't weak. Or stupid. There was something about her that bothered him. Something fishy that made him want to keep asking her questions until the answers started to make sense.

Then she asked a question of her own. "So what do you do for a living, Nate?"

"I'm a security specialist," he replied without missing a beat. "In fact, I've done some security work for Harlan—surveillance cameras around his estate and keyless entries, that sort of thing."

"Is that why he trusts you alone with me?"

"That and the fact that any significant change in your bioreadings will bring someone in here to check on you. Plus, there's the call button, which you just proved works quite well."

She leaned up to look at it and he inhaled the soft scent of her hair and felt the warmth radiating from her body. A body separated from him by only the thin fabric of her nightshirt.

He fought to keep his focus. "So you see, we're not quite as alone as it seems."

That realization dampened his impending fantasy. A fantasy that featured Carleen without her nightshirt.

Not a good idea.

In the first place, she was an engaged woman. In the second place, he had every reason to believe that she was a liar and a scam artist,. and that she was only marrying Tobias Hamilton for his fortune.

But if he did attempt to seduce her, what better way to prove her love and loyalty to Tobias? If she resisted his advances, then Nate could pass it on to Mrs. Hamilton as evidence that Carleen truly loved her son. If she didn't…then better the truth come out now rather than after the wedding.

She yawned beside him, then rolled away, tucking her pillow under her head. "I have to admit that does make me feel better. No offense, Nate."

"None taken."

Nate considered the consequences of romancing Carleen Wimmer away from Hamilton, aware of the dangers of mixing business with pleasure. And seducing this woman would most definitely be a pleasure. His body tightened just thinking about stripping away that nightshirt and discovering *all* her intimate secrets.

"Besides," she said sleepily, "if you're a security specialist, I should be safe with you."

Nate smiled into the dark at her assumption. *Big mistake, Carleen. Big mistake.*

THE NEXT MORNING, Mia awoke to find Nate hovering over her, his fingers gently brushing over her right temple. She sucked in her breath, afraid to move as his eyes met hers. Afraid not to move as he leaned toward her to whisper, "Good morning."

His smile was slow and sexy, sending her heartbeat into double time. Muscles bulged in his arm as he propped himself up on his elbow next to her. He lay so close to her that his thigh pressed into her hip and she could feel the radiant heat of his powerful body from head to toe.

An odd, tingling warmth swirled in the pit of her stomach, then moved lower. Her gaze fell to his firm lips. They were so near to her own that she could capture his mouth in a kiss without even moving her head off the pillow. Maybe that would finally quench the fire that had been burning inside of her since Nate had slipped beneath the covers last night.

He looked even better in the light of day. Dark

eyebrows arched across his wide brow and whiskers shadowed his lean jaw.

Mia saw both strength and experience in his face, which she found more alluring than any picture-perfect male model. She wanted to ask him about the scar above his right eyebrow and the second one she'd just noticed at the base of his chin. She wanted to trace the rugged terrain of his cheekbones with her fingertips as well as the small dimple that rarely dared to appear at the corner of his mouth.

She wanted what she couldn't have.

"I didn't mean to wake you," he murmured, his fingers sliding over her forehead and into her hair.

Then what had he meant to do? Seduce her in her sleep? Mia imagined waking up with his hands under his nightshirt, his nimble fingers caressing her breasts instead of her head. Or finding him naked under the sheets, his lips sliding slowly up her inner thigh until he found her wet and ready for him. *Like she was right now.*

"What are you doing?" she asked, her voice raspy with both sleep and desire.

"Hannah was in a few minutes ago and unhooked you from the machine. There's still some of that sticky gel on your forehead and in your hair. I was trying to wipe it off before it dried."

A perfectly reasonable explanation. So why did his touch feel more like a seduction than a simple act of kindness? She saw no kindness in his eyes. Only heat and hunger and a stark, raw need that touched something deep inside of her. Something that made her want him even more, if that was possible.

But it didn't matter how much she wanted him, she couldn't *have* him. Not if she finally wanted to break her bad habit of falling too hard and too fast for the wrong kind of man. And Nate Cafferty had Mr. Wrong written over every inch of his sinfully delicious body.

"Please," she began, her breath catching in her throat as his fingers trailed sensuously over the curve of her cheek and along the length of her jaw.

"Please what?" he whispered huskily.

She swallowed, drumming up every bit of willpower she possessed. "Please…stop. I think all the gel is off."

To her surprise, he did.

Nate rolled away from her and sat up on his side of the bed. He wiped his fingers on a tissue from the nightstand. Then she heard him take a long, deep breath before reaching for his duffel bag on the floor.

Maybe Harlan was right and she could trust him.

Not that Nate could trust *her*. He didn't even know her real name or identity, after all. But what did it really matter? After this sleep study ended, she'd never see the man again.

"Did you know you hog the covers?" Nate asked, pulling his T-shirt off, then tossing it in the bag.

Her mouth went dry at the way the muscles flexed over the width of his bare back and shoulders. "I do not."

"Do, too," he countered, glancing back at her with a smile.

Mia knew she should get out of bed, but she didn't want Nate watching her walk around in her old, grungy nightshirt. The first item on her agenda this morning was a trip to the store to buy new sleepwear.

She looked up to find Nate staring intently at her.

"You know," he said at last, "you don't look like a Carleen."

Mia had almost forgotten she was playing a part. The reminder was as effective as a bucket of ice water on all her forbidden fantasies about Nate.

"It's a family name," she improvised. "My grand-mother was the youngest of eight girls. Her father's name was Carl, so they called her Carleen when they realized they wouldn't have a son to name after him."

The words just kept tumbling out of her mouth, her tale growing taller by the second. *Keep it simple*, she admonished herself. The more details she gave him, the more holes he could poke in her story. She couldn't afford to have him voice any suspicions about her to Dr. Longo.

"That's interesting," he said, shifting on the bed to face her. "What about Wimmer? Is that English? German?"

He seemed unusually fascinated with her name. Or did he feel as awkward as Mia and was simply trying to make conversation? Her awkwardness was due to the fact that he was still shirtless. Fortunately, the man seemed oblivious of his effect on her.

"It's Dutch, actually," she replied, having no clue as to the origin. "Short for Van De Wimmer. My ancestors changed it when they immigrated to America."

He stared at her, as if waiting for more. But Mia had already lied enough for one morning. She rolled out of her side of the bed, taking the comforter with her. She wrapped it around her waist, then turned toward him. "I guess I'll see you tonight."

He nodded, rising to his feet and facing her across the bed. "Same time, same place."

Acutely aware that she probably didn't look her best, Mia disappeared inside Graceland to wash up. When she emerged several minutes later, Nate was gone.

Anxious to return home so she could be herself again, Mia quickly packed her overnight bag and then headed for the door. Harlan Longo met her there, looking unusually chipper for so early in the morning.

"How did you sleep, Carleen?"

"Fine," she lied, not wanting to admit that sharing a bed with Nate had kept her awake most of the night. She'd been all too aware of every breath he'd taken and every movement he'd made as he'd lain beside her in the dark.

"Good." The older man smiled. "I knew Nate wouldn't give you any trouble. He's not the kind of man to take advantage of a woman. At least, not an unwilling woman."

Those words lingered in her head as she made her way past the moat, the school bus and the chickens down to the front gate to retrieve her car. Instinct told her that Nate didn't come across many unwilling women in his life. Just like Ian.

Which was reason enough to keep her distance.

NATE KNEW it wouldn't take long for Harlan to find him. He'd just finished breakfast when his old friend walked into the dining room of the Longo estate.

"Well, how did it go?" Harlan asked, pouring himself a cup of hot tea.

"Not quite as I expected." Nate tossed his napkin onto his empty plate. "Carleen Wimmer might just be my most intriguing case yet."

Harlan pulled out a chair and sat down. "I think you're wrong about her. Carleen doesn't strike me as the type of woman who would scheme to marry for money. She's too sweet. Too pretty."

"That's how she reels in men like Tobias Hamilton," Nate replied. "Guys fall for that sweet and innocent act all the time."

Harlan arched a silver brow. "But not you?"

Nate didn't meet his gaze. "I'm just doing my job."

"That's what concerns me." Harlan set his teacup on the table. "Look, Nate, I know it's none of my business, but you're almost thirty years old. Don't make the same mistake I did by letting your work become your life. You just might live to regret it."

The light dimmed in Harlan's eyes and Nate knew he was thinking about his late wife. Those stupid public allegations about Harlan neglecting her illness had taken their toll. Few people knew that Adele Longo had refused treatment for her terminal illness, preferring to spend her last days at home with her husband.

Nate hadn't seen either one of them for years, losing contact with his foster parents shortly after his high school graduation, though he gave them all the credit for his making it that far.

His own father had left home when Nate was seven years old and his mother had turned to a whiskey bottle for comfort instead of to her only son. She was a mean drunk—taking out her anger and pain on the easiest target. Nate soon learned that words could hurt more than fists. He'd endured the pain of both, always hoping that one day his mother would realize how much he loved her. That he'd endure anything if she'd just be happy again.

Growing up, he'd spent more and more time on the streets, falling in with a neighborhood gang of tough kids. When he was thirteen years old, his mother had lost her job and they'd been threatened with eviction. So one night, Nate and his gang had burglarized a liquor store. A night that had changed his life forever.

That was the last time he'd seen his mother. She'd come to the police station the next morning, still suffering from the effects of a hangover, to tell him he was as worthless as his no-good father. Then she'd signed the formal papers terminating her parental rights. Oblivious to Nate's pleas for a second chance, she'd turned him over to the state and left him without a backward glance. Years later, he found out she eventually died of cirrhosis of the liver.

He lost his mother but he never lost the memories of the eighteen months he served in a hellhole they called the Pennsylvania Juvenile Rehabilitation Center. After that, he'd been sent into the foster care system. That's when fate had finally smiled on him—in the form of Harlan and Adele Longo.

They'd taken him in and told him that he wasn't worthless, though Nate had tested them at every turn. Adele had showered him with love, despite his surliness. Harlan had signed him up for boxing lessons as an outlet for all the rage inside of him.

Nate had been the city's Golden Gloves champion in his age group for three years in a row. He'd always refused to let anyone bring him down—not his mother, not a rival gang member and not another boxer.

It was the only way he knew how to survive.

Through his high school years, the Longos had made him part of their family. Then he'd left to join the Marines before his foster parents could discover for themselves what his mother already knew—that he simply wasn't worth it.

News of Adele Longo's death had finally brought Nate back to Philadelphia again after a ten-year absence, where he promised to stay as long as Harlan needed him. He hated watching his foster father go through the painful grieving process. That's why Nate had encouraged him to pursue his research projects, which seemed to help more than anything else.

"Is that why you put me in Carleen's bed?" Nate asked, trying to lighten the mood. "For a little romance? That wasn't part of our plan."

"Plans change," Harlan replied breezily. "I thought it was for the best."

"So is this a sleep study or a matchmaking project?"

"Can't it be both?" He smiled. "Once I met Carleen, I knew she couldn't be the kind of woman you think she is. I thought if you got a chance to know her, you'd see that for yourself."

Nate knew that Harlan put high stock in first impressions. Hell, he'd picked Nate out of a pool of juvenile delinquents and given him a home fifteen years ago. It was the first time in Nate's life that anyone had ever believed in him. Now Harlan wanted him to do the same with Carleen.

But it wasn't that simple. The woman had too many secrets. Besides, Nate had decided a long time ago that he was better off alone. He loved women, but like a boxer using fancy footwork, he knew that the best way to avoid a knock-out punch was to keep moving.

"Just give her a chance," Harlan said, reading the skepticism on his face. "You might be surprised."

"Don't get your hopes up," Nate admonished. "I'm not looking for sweet and innocent—if she *is* innocent. Besides, I don't think she likes me."

A twinkle lit Harlan's eye. "Oh, she likes you all right."

"How can you be so sure?"

"Because science doesn't lie." He rose to his feet. "Come with me and I'll show you."

Nate followed him to the control hub in the research center, where several of Harlan's assistants were busy analyzing the data gathered the night before.

"Please hand me the Wimmer file, Hannah."

Harlan's assistant dug through a stack of files on her desk, then pulled one out from the bottom. "Here you go, Dr. Longo."

"Thank you." He motioned Nate into his office. It was cluttered with books, papers, and an assortment of feather pillows left over from his last research project.

"Have a seat." Harlan handed him the file folder, then hovered at his shoulder as Nate opened it.

"Now take a look at her vitals when you got into bed with her," Harlan said

Nate glanced down at the file, noting a sudden spike in her pulse rate and respiration around the time that he joined her in the Elvis bed. "That's not exactly surprising. She thought I was an intruder. Anyone would have that reaction."

"Yes, but notice how long those levels stay elevated. Even after she falls asleep—or pretends to fall asleep."

Nate's gaze flicked from the television screen to the data report and back again. "According to this, she was awake for almost four hours after I got there."

"Which makes me believe that you definitely had an effect on her."

Nate closed the file, mentally storing the information for later use. "The only effect I want to have is closing this case. The sooner I can find out the truth about Carleen Wimmer, the better."

Harlan frowned. "You're not going to intimidate her, are you? I only agreed to set this up because you made her sound like some kind of ruthless barracuda. Now that I've actually met Carleen, I have to admit I'm having second thoughts."

So was Nate. He'd let Mrs. Hamilton's prejudices color his image of Carleen. But instead of finding a worldly schemer, she'd struck him more as a woman who didn't know the power of her own sexuality. Or if she did, had used it so skillfully that Nate was still reeling from their close encounter this morning.

He closed the folder. "Don't worry about Carleen. I'll be on my best behavior."

Harlan started to say something else, but Nate's cell phone interrupted him.

Nate looked at the number on the display panel. "I'd better take this."

"I'll give you some privacy." Harlan headed toward the door. "Go ahead and show yourself out when you're through. I need to start studying all the data from last night."

"Thanks, Harlan." He waited until the man was out the door before he answered the phone. "Hello, Mrs. Hamilton."

"I know it's early, Mr. Cafferty, but I'm quite eager for an update on my case."

"Not much has changed since yesterday."

"That's where you're wrong." Mrs. Hamilton's voice quavered. "My son called me last night. Somehow that tart convinced him to cut his trip short and come home a week early. He told me they're going to marry as soon as his plane lands."

"That doesn't give you much time to torpedo the wedding."

"You're the one running out of time," she countered. "I need dirt on Carleen Wimmer and I need it as soon as possible."

Nate swallowed a sigh, tempted to quit the case and let Mrs. Hamilton find her own dirt. But the thought of leaving Carleen behind bothered him more than he wanted to admit. Besides, he wasn't a quitter and Mrs. Hamilton had paid for his services.

"I'll see what I can do," he said at last.

"Please don't disappoint me, Mr. Cafferty," she replied. "I only have three weeks left to save my son."

He rang off, wondering how he could accelerate his investigation without arousing Carleen's suspicion. She had told him only the most superficial information about herself and her family so far. Nothing solid he could go on.

Then it hit him.

Maybe the key wasn't talking to Carleen, but someone who knew her. Someone who lived with her and worked with her on a daily basis.

Nate suddenly had an irresistible urge to redecorate the master bedroom of his home. And he knew the perfect interior designer to hire for the job.

Mia Maldonado.

4

MIA HIT morning rush-hour traffic on her way home from the Longo estate, so she was already in a bad mood when she pulled into her driveway and saw Ian Brock's shiny red pickup truck parked there.

In her haste this morning, she'd simply thrown on her clothes and left the Longo Research Center with her hair half-combed and no makeup. Not exactly the image to make Ian regret dumping her.

"About time you got here," he said, as she climbed out of her Miata. "It's almost nine."

"I'm running a little late this morning."

Ian walked with her to the front door, apparently unaffected by the awkwardness that made her drop her purse on the ground, the contents spilling out on the sidewalk.

Ian bent down to help her pick everything up, his hand finding her lip balm first. His mouth curved into a reminiscent smile.

"Strawberry Banana," he said, reading the label. "That was always my favorite flavor on you."

She remembered. Mia remembered everything about him, including how much it had shocked her when he'd dumped her for a younger woman. A nineteen-year-old model with bigger breasts and smaller hips. That had been bad enough, but even worse was how he'd treated her at the end. Brushing off her suspicions as paranoia. Making her doubt herself.

Until she'd caught him in the act. Then he'd had the gall to dump her before she could even react. That had been three months ago and his easy dismissal of her had hurt Mia to the core.

Now she wondered what she'd ever seen in the man. Compared to Nate, he was flashy and phony. Perfect hair. Perfect tan. Perfect clothes. She'd been so impressed with him and his skills as a carpenter that she'd failed to notice how impressed Ian was with himself.

Why hadn't she seen it sooner?

"I think it's past the expiration date," she said, taking the lip balm from him and tossing it into the trash can sitting near the front stoop.

Ian's brow crinkled, as if he just now noticed her disheveled appearance. "What happened to you?"

She walked briskly to the front door, the heavy tread of his work boots sounding on the sidewalk behind her. "What do you mean?"

"You look like hell."

Indignation prickled her skin. How dare he suddenly show up in her life again and start insulting her. As if he'd done nothing wrong. Never deceived her. Never hurt her. She wished he hadn't quit three months ago so she could fire him now.

Mia took a deep breath, determined not to show him that his opinion still mattered to her. And what better way than to make him think she'd found someone else.

She turned around and smiled at him. "Really? Nate seemed to like the way I looked this morning."

His gaze narrowed. "Who's Nate?"

"Nate Cafferty. A man I met last night."

"You mean…?" Ian shook his head in disbelief. "No. Not you, Mia. You're not a one-night-stand type of girl."

"You haven't seen me for almost three months, Ian," she countered. "You have no clue as to what type of girl I am anymore."

"So that's why you're late for work? That's why you look like you just tumbled out of bed?" A flush of indignation mottled his cheeks. "Because you slept with some other guy?"

Mission accomplished.

"I'm afraid that's none of your business anymore," she said evenly. "Why are you waiting out here, anyway? Carleen could have let you in."

"Nobody answered the door when I knocked," he told her as she tried to turn the knob.

"That's odd." Mia fished through her purse for her house key. "Carleen always opens up the office by eight."

"Maybe she got lucky last night, too," he sneered.

"Maybe," she said breezily, unlocking the door.

Ian's petty jealousy was a balm on her bruised heart. Her mother had always told her that living well was the best revenge. Now it seemed her mother was right. Mia suddenly felt better than she had in weeks.

All the lights were off when she stepped inside the house. "Carleen?"

There was no answer and she noticed the living room drapes hadn't been opened yet. No aroma of coffee wafted from the kitchen. Those were usually the first things Carleen did when she came downstairs in the morning.

"Carleen?" she called out again, leaving Ian behind in the living room as she checked the other rooms in the house. They were all empty, though she could tell Carleen's bed had been slept in. That made her feel a little better.

When she returned to the living room, Ian had disappeared, too. She found him in the kitchen, holding the refrigerator door open.

"Carleen probably ran down to the store for some milk," he said, perusing the meager contents. "Looks like you're getting low on supplies."

"I'm sure you didn't come over here to inventory my refrigerator," Mia said, anxious to get rid of him so she could shower.

He turned to face her. "Actually, I'm here to make you an offer. One I hope you can't refuse."

"What kind of offer?"

"A business merger, actually. What do you think about combining your design business and my carpentry business? Equal partners. All profits split 50/50 between us. And I'm anticipating big profits."

Mia was so shocked by his business proposal that she didn't know what to say. Despite everything that had happened between them, his offer did tempt her. Ian had a solid cash flow and an endless waiting list of clients. If they combined their companies, he could probably pull her out of insolvency in a month.

Mia turned and walked into the living room, her head spinning with the possibilities. This was the answer to all her financial problems. Mia's Makeovers would be a success, proving to her family once and for all that she could manage her own life.

But at what cost? She looked at Ian, suddenly wary. How could she trust him? How could she trust herself not to leap into a situation that might end in disaster? As she'd done with every man in her life, including the one standing before her.

"We've always worked well together," Ian said, taking her silence for disapproval of his idea. "And I'm tired of all the red tape at my new company. This could be the perfect solution for both of us."

"I need time to think about it," she said, mentally weighing the pros and cons in her head. Ian's carpentry skills and ability to attract customers were definite pros.

"What is there to think about?" he asked. "From what I hear, your work schedule is almost as empty as your refrigerator."

Ian's personality was a definite con.

"That's going to change soon," she told him, walking him toward the door. "We've got some ads running on the radio this week."

"That's good to hear." His jaw tightened. "I was afraid you might have become distracted by other…pursuits."

She opened the front door. "My business always comes first."

"I hope so." He stood framed in the doorway, one hand braced on the molding. "Because I happen to think we're the perfect fit, Mia. You let me do my own thing my own way." His gaze drifted lazily down her body. "I've always liked that about you."

"Goodbye, Ian," she said firmly. "I'll let you know my answer soon."

He winked at her. "I can't wait."

She stood in the doorway, watching him walk to his truck and wondering at his new attitude toward her. Had Miss Teen Bimbo dumped him? Or did the fact that another man had expressed romantic interest in her make him want to stake his claim.

It didn't really matter. He was too late. She wouldn't make the mistake of falling for him again. Funny how one night with Nate, one *platonic* night, had made her see Ian in a new light. It just reaffirmed that she couldn't trust her instincts about men. Or her hormones.

Something she'd better remember the next time she slept with Nate.

NATE LOWERED the camera and slumped further into the seat as the red pickup truck roared past him. The photos he'd just snapped of Carleen and the muscle-bound doofus on her front porch were certain to please Mrs. Hamilton, though they didn't please him.

Harlan might believe Carleen was sweet and innocent, but Nate had just seen with his own eyes the way that jerk on her porch had been looking at her and there was nothing sweet and innocent about it. Which just made him wonder what they'd been doing *inside* the house.

There was only one way to find out.

Nate climbed out of his car and walked across the street. By the time he reached the front door, he had a plan in mind. He rang the doorbell, hoping Mia Maldonado would answer it. He'd love to have some time alone with Carleen's boss so he could pump her for information.

But when the door opened, Carleen stood on the other side, her brown eyes widening in surprise. "Nate?"

He couldn't ignore the way his body reacted when he saw her. Molten heat spiraled into his groin as he remembered the way she'd felt pressed against him this morning. All soft curves and luscious skin. He should have kissed her when he'd had the chance. Instead, he'd played the gentleman, even though he'd seen the same desire reflected in her eyes.

"Hello, again," he said, fighting for control. A fight he intended to win.

"What are you doing here?"

He saw a flash of uncertainty on her face and realized what it must look like. "I'm not stalking you," he assured her. "Actually, I'm here on business."

"Oh." She opened the door wider. "Come in."

He walked inside the house, noting the clean architectural lines and the colorful Mediterranean tile on the floor. But all he could think about was pulling her down on that floor and making love to her until neither one of them could move.

Unfortunately, that wasn't part of his plan. "This is a great place."

"Thank you." She flitted nervously around the room, straightening the pillows on the sofa and picking a piece of lint off the rug. "I…I mean, Mia has put a lot of work into it."

He watched her, surprised at how aware he was of her moods after knowing her for such a short time. Earlier this morning, she'd been apprehensive and aroused. Now, she was nervous and flustered.

Because of him?

"Is Ms. Maldonado in?" he asked, looking around. "I was hoping to speak with her."

She blinked. "Why?"

He smiled at the blunt question. "I want to hire her to redecorate my bedroom."

Before she could reply, the front door swung open and a petite blonde walked inside, carrying a brown paper sack in each arm.

"*Mia,*" Carleen exclaimed, brushing past him. "Look who's here. This is Nate Cafferty, a man I met at the sleep study last night. Nate, this is my boss, *Mia Maldonado.*"

The woman peered over the grocery sacks at him, her eyes wide. "Oh. Um. Hello."

"Nice to meet you," he replied, reaching for the bags in her arms. "Here, let me take these for you."

"Thank you."

"Just set them on the kitchen counter," Carleen said, pointing the way. "If you don't mind, I need to speak with *Mia* alone for a minute."

"No problem," he replied, heading down the hallway. The kitchen decor impressed him as much as the rest of the house. Mia Maldonado was obviously a talented decorator. He just hoped she was a talented gossip, too.

He wanted to know everything about Carleen. Not just about her relationship with Toby, but details about her background and family. Something to make him understand why she was living under an alias.

When he returned to the living room, the two women had their heads together, whispering fervently to each other. He cleared his throat, causing them to jump apart.

"I didn't mean to interrupt," he said, wondering exactly what he'd interrupted. Both women seemed very tense.

"*Carleen* tells me you're looking for a decorator," Mia said.

"Yes, I'd like to redo my bedroom. Nothing too radical, just something different. Are you interested?"

Mia looked at Carleen. "I don't know if we can fit it into our schedule."

"I think we can," Carleen replied. "And I'm sure Nate won't be too demanding."

"Not at all," he assured them, sensing that Mia wanted to turn down the job. He couldn't let that happen. "It's not a big bedroom," he told her. "I don't want a lot of changes."

Carleen smiled. "Then it's settled. We'll do it."

"Are you sure this is a good idea?" Mia asked her, tucking a strand of blond hair behind her ear. "Maybe Dr. Longo doesn't want you mingling with Mr. Cafferty outside of the sleep laboratory."

"Call me Nate," he said. "And I know Harlan won't mind."

Mia looked at Carleen. "Then I guess we need to set up a date for a consultation."

"Any time works for me," he replied, wondering why Mia was so hesitant to take on the job. She was quite pretty and he usually liked blondes, but she had none of the sparkling warmth of Carleen. Nor the same luscious curves.

"How about tomorrow morning?" Carleen suggested, looking at the calendar on the desk. "We could come by your house around ten o'clock."

"Both of you?" he asked, trying to keep the disappointment out of his voice. He wanted to get Mia alone so he could grill her about Carleen.

"We *always* work together," Mia replied adamantly. "You'd be amazed at the design concepts Carleen has picked up since she started working for me. She's almost as qualified to be a decorator as I am."

"I'm always offering suggestions," Carleen said.

"And I often take them," Mia replied. "She's got great taste."

Nate watched the two women, aware of a strange undercurrent between them that he didn't understand. Not yet, anyway.

"Okay…then, I'll see you both tomorrow." He moved toward the door.

"You'll see Carleen tonight," Mia reminded him. "At the sleep lab."

"That's right." His gaze met Carleen's and a sizzle of awareness shot through him. He wanted her, plain and simple. But he needed to play it smart. Nate didn't even know her real name. Or the name of the man who had just left here.

"We can talk about what we want to do in your bedroom," Carleen said, then caught herself. "I mean, how you'd like to decorate it."

"I already have a few ideas," he said, easily picturing Carleen naked in his bed, her thick dark hair spilling over his pillow. *Keep dreamin', Cafferty. It ain't gonna happen.*

He couldn't let it happen. Not until he found out the truth about her. Because something told him she was the most dangerous opponent he'd ever faced. If he let down his guard, she'd have him KO'd before he knew what hit him.

A prospect that was simply unacceptable.

"OH, MIA, are you sure this is a good idea?" Carleen asked as soon as they were alone. "He probably suspects something already."

"No, he doesn't." Mia headed for the kitchen, still too flustered by Nate's unexpected visit to stand still. "Besides, we need the job. I'm sure we can pull this off."

Carleen followed her. "But is it worth the risk? If he finds out you're not really me and tells Longo, you'll be kicked out of the research study."

"Even if Nate did discover the truth, which he won't, we don't know for certain that he'd tell Longo." Mia started to unload the groceries, then looked up to find Carleen staring at her. "What?"

"You like him," Carleen said.

Mia shrugged. "What's not to like?"

Carleen smiled. "No, I mean, you *really* like him."

Mia set down the can of soup. "I just met him last night. I don't even know him."

But Carleen wasn't buying it. "I saw the way you two looked at each other. There's definitely something there."

Mia relished that thought for a moment and then shook her head. "He can't like me. He thinks I'm engaged."

Carleen rolled her eyes. "Like that's ever stopped a man before! They love the thrill of the chase."

Mia remembered Ian's reaction to her this morning after she'd told him about Nate. "You might be right."

"I know I'm right." Carleen placed a box of cereal in the cupboard above the stove. "Mia, you have to be careful. You know your history. I don't want you to get hurt again."

"Nothing is going to happen between us," Mia said, telling herself it was for the best. "The fact that I'm hooked up to a jukebox the entire time puts a damper on any impending romance."

Her brow crinkled. "A jukebox?"

"I'll tell you later." Mia placed the carton of milk in the refrigerator and then folded up the empty grocery sack. "Is the coffee ready?"

"Almost."

Mia grabbed two mugs and set them on the kitchen table. She didn't want to talk about Nate anymore, not when he'd occupied her thoughts from the moment he'd climbed into bed with her. "You'll never guess who was here this morning."

"Who?"

"Ian Brock."

Carleen frowned. "What did he want?"

"Believe it or not, he wants me back—but as his business partner, not his lover."

"What did you tell him?"

"I told him I'd think about it."

Carleen fumed as she picked up the coffeepot and walked to the table. "You should have told him to drill some sense into his thick head with one of his fancy power tools. I mean, you're not actually considering it, are you?"

Mia watched her pour the steaming brew into each cup. "Actually, I am. It would certainly solve all my financial problems."

Carleen sat down across the table from her. "But look at the way he treated you, Mia. The guy is scum."

"True, but a good businesswoman wouldn't let personal feelings enter into the decision."

"Are you sure you don't still have feelings for him? That you're hoping to merge more than your businesses?"

"Positive." Mia wrapped her hands around the coffee mug. "It's over. But you should have seen his reaction when I happened to mention that I'd spent the night with Nate."

"Ah," Carleen replied, comprehension dawning in her eyes. "You wanted to make Ian jealous."

She shook her head. "I wanted him to see that I had moved on. If it bothered him to think of me sleeping with another man, so much the better."

Carleen looked pensive. "Maybe you should sleep with Nate. You never know, he might be *the one*."

A thrill shot through Mia at the idea of making love with Nate Cafferty. Then common sense set in.

"I'm not about to make that kind of mistake again. It's too…painful. Besides, it's hard enough remembering I'm supposed to be you when I'm with him. Sex would just complicate things even more."

"All very logical," Carleen concurred. "But something tells me that the more time you spend with Nate Cafferty, the harder it will be to resist him. Which is all the more reason why we shouldn't redecorate his bedroom."

The telephone rang before Mia could respond. She reached over and snatched the receiver off the wall. "Good morning, Mia's Makeovers."

A hard click sounded in her ear, followed by a dial tone. "Another hang-up," she said, replacing the receiver on the cradle. "That makes at least five this week."

Carleen got up from the table and dumped the rest of her coffee in the sink. "Yes, I know."

The edge in her voice made Mia look up. "Is something wrong?"

Carleen turned around, her face pale. "I think Toby's mother is having me followed."

"What?"

"It's just a feeling I have," Carleen explained. "Nothing concrete. Just the sense that someone is watching me."

"But why would she do that?"

"I don't know. To drive me insane before I can marry her son?" Carleen wrapped her arms around her waist. "Sometimes it seems like our wedding is never going to happen."

Mia walked over to her, noting the dark circles

under her eyes. "You've got prewedding jitters, that's all. I'm sure no one is following you."

Carleen met her gaze. "Maybe you're right. I miss Toby and I'm probably just tired and stressed from planning this wedding."

"Why don't you go lie down for a while?" Mia suggested. "I can handle everything here. It's not like we've got a bunch of new clients banging down our door."

Carleen walked out of the kitchen, leaving Mia alone with her thoughts. She'd never seen her friend so shaken before. No, wait, that wasn't true. When Carleen had first moved in a year ago, she'd jumped every time a police siren had sounded or a car had backfired. She'd also checked to make sure that all the doors and windows were locked every night.

When Mia had learned that Carleen had grown up in a small town in eastern Pennsylvania before moving to Philadelphia, she'd assumed it was all part of adjusting to living in a big city. Maybe this was simply the way Carleen reacted to changes in her life. Moves were stressful. So were weddings. No doubt Carleen would feel better once Toby returned from Germany.

As Mia began putting away the rest of the groceries, her thoughts drifted once again to Nate. She wondered what he was doing the rest of the day and if he was thinking about her. Then she reminded herself that she had to go shopping for something suitable to wear to bed with him. Not too conservative. Not too sexy. Okay, maybe a little sexy. Sexy enough to make him forget that awful nightshirt he'd seen her in.

The anticipation of sleeping with him tonight

made her feel more alive than she had in weeks. She had twenty more nights to play her masquerade. He had twenty more nights to test her willpower. But there was simply too much risk involved in letting herself fall for him.

No matter how much he tempted her.

5

"I'M CARLEEN. I'm Carleen."

Mia muttered this mantra to herself all the way from the front gate of the Longo estate to the sleep lab. She carried her tote bag over her shoulder, her brand new pink pajamas inside. It had taken her three hours to find just the right style.

She'd finally settled on a deep rose pink camisole top and matching pants with a drawstring waist. The chenille fabric was wrinkleproof and just loose enough to conceal all the bulges she wanted to hide.

"My name is Carleen Wimmer," she said to herself as she reached the door to the sleep lab. "And I'm a happily engaged woman."

A fact she'd no doubt have to remind herself of quite often in the long nights to come. An engaged woman wouldn't be tempted by a man like Nate. Well, maybe she would, but she wouldn't let him see it. Her best strategy was to just ignore him. All Mia had to do was walk into the Elvis suite, change into her new pajamas and go to sleep.

But when she opened the door to the sleep lab, she stepped into a party. So much for her strategy.

A Mexican mariachi band played in the center hub

of the room. The chrome countertops were filled with platters of tantalizing appetizers. Small knots of people filled the room, talking, laughing and even dancing. Hannah, Dr. Longo's lab assistant, stood behind a makeshift bar, salting margarita glasses and serving shots of tequila with lime.

"You're late," Nate said from behind her. "The party started almost two hours ago."

She turned to face him and the truth hit her in the solar plexus. She'd never last twenty nights. Not with this man. She'd be lucky to last twenty minutes if he kept looking at her like that. "Nobody told me about a party."

"Really?" A brow arched in surprise. "I'm sure it was mentioned in the information packet that Harlan sent out."

"Oh, right," she replied, wondering what else Carleen had neglected to tell her about. But her friend's forgetfulness wasn't surprising in her currently fragile state. Mia just hoped Carleen could relax enough to enjoy what was supposed to be the happiest time of her life.

"Let me get you something to drink," he offered. "They're serving strawberry margaritas, banana daiquiris and a wicked tequila sunrise."

"I'd love a strawberry margarita," she said, hoping the alcohol content would help her fall asleep more quickly tonight than she had the night before. Though she'd been dragging all day, she now felt a strange energy buzzing through her. She decided to attribute it to the beat of the mariachi band rather than the man standing beside her.

He tilted his head. "I thought you were allergic to strawberries."

Mia swallowed a groan. She *knew* Carleen was allergic to strawberries. How many more mistakes could she make before she got caught? *I'm Carleen Wimmer.*

"You're right, I am allergic," she replied, raising her voice as the band launched into a bolero. "So I'd better not risk it. I'll have a tequila sunrise instead."

He nodded, apparently undisturbed by her slipup. "One tequila sunrise coming up."

She watched him walk toward the bar, then went to set her tote bag inside the Elvis suite. When she emerged, she found a short, bald man with black-rimmed glasses waiting for her.

"Hi, neighbor," he said with a wide smile.

"Hello."

"I'm Glenn Hobbs." He hitched his thumb over his shoulder. "I sleep right next door."

"So you're one of the research subjects?"

"That's right." Glenn licked the salt off his empty margarita glass. "Great party, isn't it?"

Mia nodded, her gaze slowly scanning the room to observe the other guests. There were about twelve people in all, half of them women and half men. She guessed that only three or four of them were in her age range. The rest seemed to be closer to Harlan's age. Perhaps they were friends or acquaintances. Or maybe they needed the stipend money to supplement their retirement income.

"So what's your angle?" Glenn asked.

She blinked, taken aback by his question. "What do you mean?"

"I mean, how does old Harlan have you sleeping at night? Me, I'm sleeping on a straw mat on a floor of sand. No sheets. No blankets. No pillows." He reached up to rub the back of his neck. "Kind of a strain, I'll tell ya."

"Don't you get cold?"

He shook his head. "Nope. The room is set up like a tropical paradise, with a balmy temperature to match. There are real palm trees in there. A sound machine emitting ocean waves. Even a tiki hut that doubles as a biomonitor. You'd have to see it to believe it."

"Oh, I believe it," she replied, thinking of her Elvis suite. "Dr. Longo seems to take pride in making his research subjects as comfortable as possible."

Glenn snorted. "Dr. Longo is a fruitcake. But a generous fruitcake."

He held up his empty glass. "Looks like it's time for a refill."

She watched him head off to the bar and then saw Nate approaching her. Her heart tripped in her chest and she took a deep breath. *I'm Carleen. I'm Carleen.*

"Sorry it took so long," he said, handing her a glass with a tiny purple umbrella in it. "There was a line at the bar for upside-down margaritas."

She sipped her drink, refreshed by the cool citrus flavor. "Exactly what is an upside-down margarita?"

Nate smiled. "You walk up to the bar, tip your head back on top of it, and then the bartender pours tequila, triple sec and lime into your mouth straight from the bottles."

She laughed. "Harlan really knows how to throw

a party. I'm not quite sure how it will affect his research, though. Won't alcohol skew the results?"

Nate shrugged. "Something tells me Harlan's research isn't always as clear-cut as it seems."

That seemed obvious to her, but she still liked the
man. She took another sip of her drink, surprised at
how easily it went down.

"Do you want some nachos?" he offered, moving
toward the counter.

"Maybe just one." She scooped up a chip off the
platter, rich with guacamole and sour cream. It broke
in half as she brought it to her mouth and tumbled
off her chin.

Nate caught it with an outstretched hand, then
popped it into his mouth. He chewed, then said,
"Pretty good."

She smiled up at him. "Maybe we should design
a Mexican theme for your bedroom. Minus the mariachi band."

"Now there's an idea." He laughed. "But let's
leave the decorating to your boss. She's the professional, after all."

Mia nodded, then dropped her gaze to her glass.
I'm Carleen. I'm Carleen.

Why was that so hard to remember when Nate
was around? Granted, the man was gorgeous, but
that was no excuse. He was also smart, and if she
didn't get it together he was going to figure out she
wasn't Carleen. Something told her he wasn't a man
who liked to be fooled.

But then, who did?

Harlan entered the room and clapped his hands to

get their attention. The music faded away and the band began to pack up their instruments.

"Time for bed," Harlan announced.

A collective groan filled the room.

"I know you're all having fun," Harlan said. "But we still have a research study to conduct and it's getting late. Those of you standing in line at the bar can take your drinks back to your suites. For the rest of you, Hannah might be a while filling drink orders before she can hook you up, so please be patient."

Nate sighed as they walked toward the Elvis suite. "Harlan has lousy timing. I was just about to ask you to dance."

Mia opened the door and they stepped inside, greeted by the strains of Elvis singing "You Don't Know Me."

"So what's stopping you?" she asked impulsively. "We've got our own music right here."

He smiled. "You're absolutely right."

Nate took the drink from her hand and set it on a small table in the shape of an old 45 record before pulling her into his arms.

That's when Mia knew she'd made a big mistake. Because it seemed so natural to circle her arms around his waist and let him pull her close against him. She could feel the palms of his broad hands pressed against her lower back, their warmth seeping through her blouse. Their bodies moved together in perfect rhythm, swaying to the seductive cadence of the love song.

She tried to think of all the reasons not to let Nate hold her this way, but they evaporated when he tilted his head down and met her gaze. Mia's instincts told her he was going to kiss her. Those same instincts told her she wasn't going to do a damn thing to stop him. She didn't want to stop him—and that was the simple truth of the matter.

He lowered his head, his mouth just a hairbreadth from her own. Anticipation welled up inside of her, making her heart pound harder than a drum. Her legs grew wobbly beneath her and she leaned into his body for support. But he still didn't kiss her, stretching the moment out to unbearable lengths.

Mia finally ended the sensual torment herself, closing the infinitesimal distance between them until their lips met. The intimate contact seemed to shatter Nate's control and he crushed her against him in a soul-rending kiss that sent her senses spinning.

She savored his passionate response, gratified to know she wasn't the only one half-crazed with lust. The scorching pressure of his mouth ignited flames of desire that licked at her breasts and her inner thighs and the soles of her feet.

Mia had never been kissed by a man like this before and doubted she ever would be again. All the more reason to savor these few fleeting moments before she had to remind herself why Nate was all wrong for her.

As if he sensed her inner struggle, his kiss suddenly gentled, though his arms didn't loosen around her. He gently nibbled the soft flesh of her lips between her teeth, sipping her soft moans as if they were nectar. At last, he lifted his head and stared into her eyes.

"Wow," was all he said.

She stepped away from him, taking several deep breaths before she could speak. "How did that happen?"

"I'm not sure," he replied, looking as perplexed as she felt. "Maybe the party. The tequila. The music. Or a combination of all three."

She nodded, all the while knowing none of those things could account for the intensity of that kiss. "We just got carried away."

"It happens," he concurred.

Mia wanted to ask him if a kiss like that had ever happened to him before, but thought better of it. Instead, she reached down and grabbed her tote bag off the floor. "I'm going to change now."

When she emerged from Graceland, Nate was already in bed.

"Nice pajamas," he said, watching her walk toward him.

"Thank you." Her legs still felt a little wobbly, but she made it to the bed, settling onto her side and pulling the gold lamé comforter up to her chin.

A moment later, the lights flicked off.

"How do they do that?" she asked, willing to say anything to break the tension sizzling between them.

"There's a sensor in all the beds that measures the weight," he explained. "When your weight is added to my weight, the lights go off. Everything is automated here. For instance, the jukebox starts to play when the door is opened. Although the lab assistants can override any part of the system."

If only she could do the same with her body. How

could she lie so close to Nate and not touch him? Especially when everything inside of her still thrummed with the primal need his kiss had evoked?

Mia knew she had two choices. She could repeat the same mistake she'd made so many times in the past or she could pretend that kiss had never happened.

She turned to face him in the dark, the glow of the jukebox illuminating his face, and made her choice. "How do you know so much about this place?"

"I used to live here," he relied evenly. "Harlan and Adele Longo were my foster parents."

"Oh." She didn't know how to ask him more without sounding nosy.

But Nate sensed her curiosity. "They took me in when I was fifteen and didn't have anywhere else to go. Harlan is the closest thing to a father that I've ever had."

She was touched that he'd share such a personal part of his life with her. "He seems like a good man."

"One of the best," Nate replied and then lightened the moment with a smile. "Except when he turns me into one of his guinea pigs."

She laughed. "I hope this study isn't too torturous for you."

His gaze lingered on her face. "Torturous is the perfect word to describe it. Harlan knows how to make a man suffer."

Nate's meaning had been clear, but she didn't know how to react. Dare she admit her own attraction to him? Before Mia could reply, the door opened and the overhead lights flicked on.

Hannah walked into the room. "Time to hook you up to the jukebox, Carleen."

She welcomed the interruption and the extra security measure the jukebox biomonitor would provide her. Nate likely wouldn't want to kiss her again while she was hooked up to the machine and she couldn't reach his side of the bed with the cable wires attached to her.

She lay still as the lab assistant applied the small adhesive pads to her temples and forehead, then hooked the cables to them. Nate watched the process, making her more self-conscious than ever about how she must look hooked up to this contraption.

"So tell me more about Harlan's laboratory," Mia said, after Hannah had left them alone again.

Nate propped himself up on his elbow and lay facing her. "He built it shortly after the death of his wife. I think he needed something to distract him from his grief. Because he suffered from insomnia, that's the area he wanted to explore."

"This place is very impressive."

"State of the art."

"But does anyone actually take his work seriously?" she asked. "Anyone in the scientific community?"

Nate rolled onto his back and folded his arms behind his head. The position emphasized the sleek muscles in his arms and shoulders. "I doubt it. Probably because he gets more press than they do."

Mia barely heard him. She was too distracted by the raw power emanating from him. Then he turned toward her, his bare leg brushing against her knee.

She pulled it back too fast, every nerve in her body

jumping at the contact. "Sorry. I must be taking up too much room. I'm not used to sleeping with someone."

He arched a brow. "Even your fiancé?"

Her fiancé. She'd forgotten all about her supposed engagement. What must Nate think of her after that kiss?

"We're waiting," she improvised, trying to cover her tracks, "until after the wedding."

"Interesting," he mused, giving her no clue as to his thought processes.

Maybe Carleen was right and he did see an unavailable woman as a challenge. *The thrill of the chase.* That might be the only reason he'd kissed her back tonight.

The sound of a cell phone ringing disrupted her thoughts. The ring was muffled and came from the far corner of the room.

"I think that's mine," Mia said, realizing she'd left the cell phone in her tote bag. She couldn't reach it without detaching all the cable wires.

"Do you want me to get it for you?"

"Please."

Nate climbed out of bed and a moment later the overhead lights flicked on. He padded in his bare feet over to her tote bag, looking deliciously rumpled in his faded gray T-shirt and black cotton shorts. He bent down and began to unzip the bag.

"It's in the side pocket," she told him, as the cell phone rang for the fourth time.

Nate pulled it out, then looked at the display window. "The caller ID says Ian Brock. Do you want to take it?"

She hesitated. "Sure."

He handed her the phone, then climbed back into bed. The lights flicked off again as she flipped opened the cell phone.

"Hello?"

"Hello, creampuff."

She cringed at Ian's old nickname for her, as well as the fact that he spoke so loudly Nate could probably hear every word. "Why are you calling me?"

"I just wanted to hear your voice. After we talked this morning, I couldn't stop thinking about you."

"Oh." She wasn't sure what to say to him, especially with Nate listening in.

"Have lunch with me tomorrow?"

"Why?"

Ian's deep chuckle carried over the line. "Do we need a reason to have lunch together? We're still friends, aren't we?"

That got her blood up. "I'm not so sure I'd go that far."

"Look, I've made mistakes," Ian replied. "I'll be the first one to admit it."

That was big of him.

"Just give me a chance," Ian continued. "We can talk about our proposed business venture. I have some figures I think you should see before you make a decision."

He had a point. She could at least him hear out. Besides, watching Ian grovel might prove entertaining—and help take her mind off of Nate. "When and where?"

"How about Cavalli's?" he suggested, naming her favorite Italian restaurant. "Say around one o'clock."

"That should work for me."

"I can't wait. See you tomorrow."

She cut off the connection and then set the cell phone on the floor beside the bed, intensely aware of Nate watching her.

"So who's Ian?"

Mia laid back on her pillow, telling herself to stick to the truth as much as possible. She was much less likely to be tripped up that way. "He's an old friend."

"As in old boyfriend?"

"Yes." Mia turned away from him, bunching her pillow under her cheek. She hoped he'd get the hint and stop asking questions.

"So what does your fiancé think about Ian?"

Mia mentally kicked herself. She kept forgetting she was supposed to be engaged. No doubt Nate wondered why she was taking calls from an old boyfriend. He might have even overheard Ian invite her to lunch.

"We've never really talked about him," Mia said at last.

"Don't most couples talk about their old loves?"

She decided to go on the offensive. Rolling over to face him, she said, "I don't know. Do you?"

"I've never been engaged."

"But you've been in relationships, right? So how do you handle it?"

"I don't kiss and tell." His gaze fell to her mouth. "You can trust me on that, Carleen."

That was the problem. She couldn't trust him or herself. That one kiss had proved to Mia how easy it would be to fall into his arms. A trip she couldn't afford to take.

She forced herself to turn away from him, an empty ache in her chest. "Goodnight, Nate."

"Goodnight, Carleen."

She lay in the darkness, listening to Elvis and thinking about what would have happened if she hadn't turned away. If she'd reached out to touch him instead, sliding her hand over his broad chest and taut belly. If she'd slipped her fingers beneath the waistband of his black cotton shorts to cup the thick arousal that had been so plainly visible when he'd gotten up to retrieve her cell phone.

Then Mia closed her eyes and told herself not to think anymore.

6

NATE PUNCHED the leather training bag hanging from the rafter in his basement. In his youth, he'd worked out his anger by beating on a heavy bag like this until his knuckles bled. Now he worked out a different kind of frustration. One that came from sleeping next to a woman without making love to her. And he definitely wanted to make love to Carleen.

He pounded the bag again, telling himself she shouldn't have this kind of effect on him. She was not only engaged to be married, but lying about her identity. Two facts that had meant absolutely nothing to him when he'd kissed her last night.

Or rather, when she'd kissed him.

The wait had been worth it. He'd almost burst a blood vessel in those agonizing moments when his lips had hovered over hers, waiting for her to make the first move. Moments that had stretched into an eternity, tearing his willpower to shreds.

She'd surrendered to the inevitable only a fraction of a second before he'd been about to do the same, proving him right in the process. A woman with that much passion didn't belong with a spineless wimp like Tobias Hamilton. The guy might have money, but she needed more. She needed a man who could satisfy her.

And that was a job Nate was willing to take on for free.

The doorbell rang and he hurled one last solid punch at the bag before heading up the stairs. He loosened the laces of his boxing gloves with his teeth as he headed toward the front door, tugging off the one on his right hand so he could open it.

Carleen stood on the other side, looking so fresh and cool and beautiful that he felt like a big, slobbering idiot staring at her. Then he noticed the way she was staring at him and looked down to see himself wearing only a sheen of perspiration and a pair of royal blue boxing trunks that had seen better days.

An appreciative smile curved on her lips when she lifted her gaze to meet his once again. "Looks like I'm early."

He glanced at the clock on the wall as he opened the door far enough to her to come in. "Actually, you're right on time. Where's your boss?"

"Mia is supposed to meet me here," she replied, stepping inside. "She's always very punctual."

He removed the boxing glove from his left hand, then grabbed a folded towel off the coffee table that doubled as his laundry center and started wiping himself down.

She watched him for a moment, then cleared her throat and let her gaze wander over the living room. "This is nice."

"I like it."

There was a tension between them that hadn't

been there before, each too aware of the tinderbox nature of their relationship. It was entirely possible that another kiss could spark a blaze of passion that neither of them could control.

Nate just had to decide if he wanted to risk it.

"Well, we might as well get busy," he said, tossing the towel aside. "My bedroom is this way."

ALARM BELLS clanged inside of Mia's brain as she followed him through the living room. This was exactly the type of situation she needed to avoid. It was hard enough resisting Nate in the sleep lab. But here, alone in his house, with him dressed in a pair of snug boxing trunks that left nothing to the imagination, she was in serious danger.

Not from him, but from herself.

It was all too easy to imagine following him into his bedroom and divesting him of those shorts. Then she could slowly lick the salty sweet skin that beckoned her now, making her ache to touch and taste him everywhere.

"Is something wrong?"

Her fantasy evaporated and she found herself in the doorway to Nate's bedroom, both hands braced against the frame. "Just a little dizzy," she replied, dropping her hands and stepping inside his room.

The spacious bedroom was starkly furnished, with only a king-size bed and one lone dresser. Like the living room, the walls were painted white and the oak floor was bare of throw rugs. The bed was neatly made, with white sheets beneath a plain gray coverlet.

"As you can see, I'm not much of a decorator—"

he bent down and scooped up a lone sock off the floor "—or much of a cleaner."

"Don't worry about it." Her mind danced with possibilities. The bedroom was like a blank canvas and she couldn't wait to bring it to life with some color and texture. "A good designer wants to see how you live so she can design a room that best fits your style."

A dimple popped up on one side of his mouth. "How do you think your boss will describe my style?"

She thought about it for a moment. He didn't fit any of the traditional design styles. Nate was a warrior. A man ready to pack up and go off to battle at a moment's notice. The sparse furnishings in his home and the lack of pictures on his walls proved that mobility was important to him.

Which reinforced Mia's belief that Nate was all wrong for her. She wanted more than a temporary man in her life. At twenty-eight, she wanted something more permanent. Even if it meant settling for bland.

Nate Cafferty could never be bland.

But he could be one last fling. The thought popped unbidden into her head. She tried to ignore it, but watching Nate bend down to retrieve the other sock from under his bed made her consider the possibility.

What if she went into a relationship with Nate knowing it was temporary? The sleep study would be over in nineteen days. She could spend those nineteen days—and nights—with her fantasy man. Quench her desire for the ultimate Mr. Wrong once and for all. Then the two of them could part ways without acrimony and she could move on with her life with no regrets. And she'd have a few pleasant memories to dust off and enjoy during her golden years with Mr. Bland.

It seemed like the perfect plan. Too perfect. Mia refused to let herself act on it until she'd given it some more thought. Especially when it was almost impossible to think rationally with Nate in his current state of undress.

"Your style," she mused, remembering the question he'd asked before she'd become sidetracked. "I'd call it eclectic."

He laughed. "Isn't that just a nice way of saying chaotic?"

"Not at all," she countered. "Eclectic blends a number of different styles into one space. I see both antique and modern pieces here, Americana and Asian influences. To be honest, the diversity intrigues me."

Nate *intrigued* her. She found herself even more curious about the man after seeing his home. Mia had almost driven by it on the way over, surprised to find him living in a circa 1940s' house with cheerful yellow siding, green shutters and a white picket fence around the yard.

Even more surprising were the neatly clipped rosebushes in the front yard. She couldn't see Nate having the patience to care for rosebushes. In fact, she couldn't see Nate living in this vintage neighborhood. It was more suited to a little old lady than a tough guy like him.

"I picked up a few things in the Philippines when

I was in the Marines," he said. "Some of them are still in storage."

"I thought most Marines have a tattoo," she teased. "I read somewhere that it's almost a rite of passage for new recruits."

"That's true," he replied, "but my mother hated tattoos. I made her a promise when I was ten years old that I'd never get one."

His loyalty touched her. "I bet she was very proud of you."

"You'd lose that bet."

When he didn't elaborate, Mia realized she'd inadvertently stumbled into dangerous territory. An emotional minefield that she didn't understand. Judging by the implacable expression on Nate's face, he wasn't about to explain it to her.

But when he spoke again, the bitterness in his voice had vanished. "So did you pass on that Mexican theme idea to Mia? I think it has definite possibilities."

She smiled. "Actually, I haven't seen her since yesterday. I'm surprised she's not here yet." She glanced at her watch. "Maybe I should try to call her."

"That reminds me," Nate said. "I need to apologize for last night."

For a moment, she thought he was talking about the kiss and her stomach lurched in dismay. "Apologize?"

"I probably got a little too personal," he continued. "That telephone call was your business. I don't have the right to question you about Ian Brock or your fiancé or any other man in your life."

"Don't worry about it," she said, feeling like she was on a roller-coaster ride.

"Well, if I ever get too personal, just tell me to back off."

Mia looked up at him, thinking that the last thing she wanted Nate to do was back off. "I will."

The doorbell rang and she knew Carleen had finally arrived. "That must be my boss."

Mia let her into the house while Nate changed out of his boxing trunks. By the time she escorted Carleen back to the bedroom, he was dressed in khaki slacks and a polo shirt.

"The place is all yours," Nate told them, stepping aside to allow them both a better view of the room.

Carleen took a slow turn around and then looked at Mia. "Are you thinking what I'm thinking?"

Mia bit back a smile at the leading question. "That depends. Are you thinking of splashing the room with color? We could start with meridian or even a chartreuse paint on the walls. Then go with a taupe Berber rug for the floor and Roman shades for all of the windows."

Carleen nodded. "Exactly." Then she turned to Nate. "How does that sound?"

He shook his head. "Since I don't recognize half the words you just said, I think I'm out of my element here. I'll leave all the decisions in your capable hands."

"Don't worry," Mia reassured him. "I think you'll be satisfied."

He met her gaze with a look that told her he wasn't thinking about decorating. "I think I will be, too."

Carleen looked between the two of them and then cleared her throat. "Well, what should we do next?"

Mia reached for her tote bag. "I'm sure you'll want to take some measurements before we get started."

Carleen took the tape measure from her. "You read my mind again. Nate, can you help me measure the windows?"

While the two of them took measurements, Mia wrote down all the dimensions they called out.

When the telephone rang, Nate was perched on a chair measuring the ceiling for a custom molding. "Can you get that for me, Carleen?"

It took Mia a moment to realize he was talking to her. She picked up his cell phone off the nightstand and flipped it open. "Hello?"

"To whom am I speaking?" asked a female voice. Mia hesitated.

"I'm with the decorator."

"Where is Mr. Cafferty?"

She glanced up to see Nate stretched precariously toward the far corner. "He's occupied at the moment. May I take a message?"

"Tell him to unoccupy himself. I have urgent business to discuss with him."

Mia placed her palm over the receiver. "A woman wants to talk to you, Nate. She said it's urgent."

He grumbled under his breath, then retracted the tape measure and climbed down from the chair before taking the phone from her. "Hello?"

Mia watched him, wondering if it was one of his clients on the other end of the line. Or possibly a girlfriend, though the voice on the phone sounded like an older woman. They'd talked about relationships last night, but he hadn't mentioned anyone special in his life.

Nate looked up and caught Mia staring at him. "Excuse me for a minute," he said, then backed into the bathroom and closed the door.

"Well," Carleen chimed, "I guess he wants some privacy. Which gives me the perfect opportunity to ask what happened between you two last night."

"Nothing happened," Mia replied. "And nothing is going to happen. Not when we're practically under a microscope in that sleep lab."

"So does that mean you'd like something to happen?"

"No. Maybe. I don't know." Mia was more confused than ever. "Besides, there's Ian."

Carleen wrinkled her nose. "What does *he* have to do with anything?"

"Well, it hasn't been that long since we broke up— only three months. I don't want to fall for someone on the rebound."

"Three months is like three years in rejection land," Carleen informed her. "I think a man like Nate is exactly what you need to make you forget Ian."

Before she could respond, Nate emerged from the bathroom, apologizing for taking so long.

"I think we're finished here anyway," Carleen said. "Aren't we, *Carleen?*"

Mia blinked. "Oh. Right. Yes, we're finished."

Carleen turned to Nate. "We'll get back to you when we're ready to start. I'll let Carleen work out the details with you so you're not inconvenienced too much."

"Sounds good," Nate ran a hand through his hair, still slightly damp from his workout. It curled slightly at the ends and Mia wondered if that's why he kept it cut so short.

"Then we'll see you soon," Carleen promised, moving toward the living room.

Mia turned to follow her, but Nate grasped her hand and stopped her in her tracks.

"One more thing," he said, reaching into the pocket of his slacks. "I'm always in and out, so you'll need a house key."

He turned her hand over and placed a key in her palm. Then he grinned. "Guess I don't have to worry about you breaking in here in the middle of the night to ravish me since we're already sleeping together."

Her heart skipped a beat at the thought of ravishing him. "Your key and your virtue are safe with me."

Mia wasn't quite sure how to interpret the pained look on Nate's face as he let her out the door.

THREE HOURS LATER, Nate sat in his car outside Cavalli's restaurant. He'd seen Carleen go inside five minutes ago and he found himself hoping her old boyfriend would stand her up. Then Nate spotted a familiar red pickup truck pulling into the lot and realized he wouldn't be so lucky.

Nothing had gone right today.

Carleen had shown up at his house for the design consultation before Mia, torpedoing his plan to dig for some information about her. He cringed at the thought of how he must have looked to Carleen—all sweaty and raunchy in his boxing trunks.

Then Beatrice Hamilton had called, demanding another progress report. He just hoped she hadn't spilled anything when Carleen had answered his phone. Something told him Beatrice was smarter than that. He'd learned a long time ago that the most ruthless people in life were the most detached—never letting their emotions interfere with their judgment.

His mother had been like that the day she'd turned him over to the state. Cold. Unemotional. Almost robotlike, in spite of her hangover. He'd watched her sign the official form severing their relationship as if she'd been signing a postal receipt. Not even pausing to consider all the ramifications. Simply ridding herself of an inconvenience. A disposable son.

Now he needed to detach himself from this case. Or at least keep a tight rein on his feelings and not allow his strong attraction to Carleen to get in the way of the investigation.

He shouldn't care if she was seeing her old boyfriend on the side. In fact, it would make Nate's job a hell of a lot easier. All he'd have to do is snap a few pictures of them together during an intimate moment and Beatrice Hamilton would have all the ammunition she'd need to stop the wedding.

Nate watched Ian walk into the restaurant, noting his cocky stride and his perfectly pressed navy slacks. Just the thought of that man holding Carleen made his gut twist inside of him. So much for cold detachment.

Nate climbed out of his car, grabbing a newspaper off the front seat before he followed Ian inside. The restaurant was dark, but he kept his sunglasses on and a ball cap pulled low over his brow. He scanned the crowded room, finally spotting Carleen and her date in a secluded corner. They looked very cozy.

Nate took a seat at the bar, holding the newspaper in front of him, but just low enough to keep his eyes on the couple. It looked like Ian was doing most of the talking, but Carleen didn't seem to mind. She had changed from the professional black suit she'd worn to his house this morning into a knockout blue dress.

"What can I get for you?" the bartender asked him, wiping down the counter with a wet rag.

"I'll take an iced tea."

"Would you like to see a menu?"

He shook his head, surprised to find he didn't have any appetite. Then his gaze was drawn to the corner table again. He saw Ian reach out and take Carleen's hand. She let him hold it for a moment, then withdrew it to pick up her menu.

The more Nate watched the two of them, the more confused he became. She didn't seem comfortable with the man, so why sneak out on her fiancé with him? It didn't make sense.

Was Ian coercing her in some way? Blackmailing her? That was a definite possibility, since Carleen Wimmer was using an alias. Maybe Ian knew her secrets, but demanded a price of money or sex or both to keep his silence.

So what exactly was she trying to hide?

Nate had never hit so many brick walls before in an investigation. Usually, there was some loose thread that he could pick up on. But Carleen Wimmer, or whoever she was, had covered her tracks well.

Which left only one way for him to discover her

secrets. He needed her to trust him. That's why he'd given her the house key this morning. It was also the reason he'd apologized for commenting on her telephone call from Ian last night.

But earning someone's trust was a slow process. Hell, it had taken the Longos almost three years to earn Nate's trust. He had less than three weeks—which made him reconsider his hesitation to sleep with Carleen. That kind of intimacy engendered trust almost immediately.

Besides, she didn't belong with Tobias Hamilton. Even if she did care for the man, Beatrice would embark on a lifelong mission to make both their lives miserable. He'd save Carleen a lot of grief and heartache if he stepped in now, before it was too late.

Nate was honest enough to admit to himself that he wouldn't be sleeping with Carleen for purely unselfish reasons. He wanted to slake this thirst for her—a thirst that was almost turning into an obsession. He'd never wanted a woman as much as he wanted her.

"Here you go, sir." The bartender set the iced tea in front of him.

Nate dug a five-dollar bill out of his wallet and laid it on the bar. Then he picked up the frosty glass and took a long sip, letting the tea wash down his throat. When he looked at Carleen and Ian again, she was laughing, a pretty pink blush on her cheeks. Jealousy rose within him, swift and hot.

He'd had enough.

He folded the newspaper, tucking it under his arm before leaving the bar. Out in the sunlight once more, he walked straight to Ian's pickup truck. Nate peered into the front seat, noting the black leather interior and premium stereo system. The guy definitely had money. After pulling a stubby pencil from his pocket, he jotted down the license plate number on the blank edge of the newspaper.

Maybe finding out more about her old boyfriend would lead him to the truth about Carleen. If she was scamming Tobias Hamilton, the two of them might be in it together. Time to find out if good old Ian had a prison record or if he'd ever been in any other trouble with the law.

Time for Nate to get ruthless.

7

"DID I TELL YOU how beautiful you look today?" Ian asked, gazing at her from across the table.

"At least three times," Mia replied, surprised to find herself growing irritated with him. She used to glow for days from one of his rare compliments. Now they seemed phony and forced. Had he changed that much or had she?

"I'm glad this place is running behind today," he said. "It gives us more time together."

She glanced at her watch. "Don't you have to get back to work soon?"

He waved away her concern. "I'm not worried about it. The last thing the company wants to do is fire their best carpenter. They've learned that I take orders from no one."

She looked around the crowded restaurant, hoping to see the waiter headed in their direction. A movement at the bar caught her attention and for a moment she thought she saw Nate. Then he was gone and she told herself it must be wishful thinking.

She'd been seeing Nate a lot lately. In her bed. In her dreams. Most recently, in a pair of skimpy boxing trunks. That sight had been enough to whet her appetite for more.

"I have a confession to make," Ian said, jolting her back to the present. "Tina was a mistake. I realized that about two seconds after I started dating her. Too self-absorbed and immature. Only concerned about her own wants. That's why I dumped her."

Mia sat back in her chair, unable to guess what he was going to say next.

"I've decided I want you back in my life again, Mia. You're smart and sexy. A woman who needs me as much as I need her."

"Ian, I…"

"No," he interjected, holding up both hands. "Don't say anything. Not yet. Let me have my say. Then I just want you to think about it. Think about all the great times we had together."

The waiter chose that moment to appear at the table. "Who had the halibut?"

"That's mine," Mia said, picking up her napkin as he set the plate in front of her.

"Then you must be the ham," the waiter said and Ian shot him a dirty look. "Careful of that plate. It's hot, hot, hot."

The waiter stepped back from the table. "Can I get you anything else?"

"Just some privacy," Ian hinted.

He waited until the waiter was out of sight, then turned his attention back to Mia. "Now, where were we…."

She picked up her fork.

"You were telling me how great we were together."

His mouth curved into a smile. "That's right. You can't deny it, Mia. Those were some hot times."

The halibut was flaky and moist, but she had to force herself to eat it. What was she doing here with Ian? The more time she spent with him, the less she liked him. He was a walking definition of self-absorbed.

All the more reason to seduce Nate. He'd be the perfect man to make her forget about Ian and the months she'd wasted with him. Nate didn't need to tell her she was sexy—he made her feel sexy. Intuition told her he'd be an unselfish lover. The one kiss they'd shared told her they were made for each other. In bed, anyway.

"Mia?" he prodded, breaking her reverie. "Do you miss those times as much as I do?"

"That's all in the past," she said, dodging the question. "I thought we were here to talk about the future. You mentioned something about some figures over the phone."

"Oh, right." He pulled a sheet of paper from his shirt pocket. "I threw together a projected cash flow to reflect the financial impact of combining our companies. If we started sharing overhead expenses, like office space and administrative services, we could save a considerable amount of money."

She studied his proposal, stunned by the numbers in front of her. This venture would do more than save her from insolvency—it would potentially make her a rich woman some day—if it was accurate. "May I take this home with me and study it for a while?"

"Please do," he replied. "Perhaps we should get together Saturday night and talk about it some more. I'll bring the wine."

"Ian," she began, "I'm not ready to start dating you again."

"Of course you're not," he concurred. "I messed up. Now I have to find a way to make it right. We'll start slowly, putting our businesses together, then go from there."

She didn't seem to be getting through to him. Ian heard what he wanted to hear. Despite the figures she'd just seen, rekindling a relationship with Ian, even a business relationship, sent up all kinds of red flags.

After all, she was convinced that the only reason he wanted her back was to soothe his ego now that he believed she'd found someone else. "This Saturday night won't work for me."

"How about next Saturday night?"

"I already have plans."

A muscle twitched in his jaw. "So you're still seeing that guy?"

"Every night."

His eyes narrowed as he gave her a cool smile. "I'm not afraid of a little competition."

She laid her napkin on her plate, done with lunch and with this conversation. "I need to go. Thank you for lunch, Ian. I'm still interested in possibly working with you, but the boyfriend position isn't available anymore."

Ian followed her out of the restaurant and into the lobby. "I don't give up that easily, Mia. We'll talk soon."

"Goodbye, Ian."

She could feel his gaze on her all the way to her car. Ian was possessive and no doubt saw her as his and his alone. If she was lucky, he'd meet up with another teenage bimbo soon and forget about her.

If she was lucky, Nate Cafferty would make her forget Ian had ever existed.

THAT NIGHT, Nate walked into the Elvis suite and found Carleen already hooked up to the jukebox. Even with all those cables sticking out of her head, she was sexy as hell. Looked like he had another night in purgatory to look forward to—consigned to sleeping next to the most desirable woman he'd ever met without touching her.

She looked up from the large book in her lap when he closed the door.

"You're reading in bed," he observed. "Does that mean the honeymoon's over?"

She smiled. "I brought Mia's portfolio so you could see some of the other rooms she's designed and pick your favorites. That will give me…her…I mean, us, a good idea of what types of decor appeal to you."

"Good idea," he affirmed, grateful for anything that might keep his mind occupied for a few minutes. "Let me get changed and I'll be ready to browse."

He emerged from the Graceland bathroom a short while later. The minty taste of toothpaste lingered on his tongue and the memory of Carleen laughing with Ian during their intimate lunch that afternoon lingered in his mind.

He wanted to make her forget Ian Brock and Tobias Hamilton and every other man she'd ever known. Selfish as it sounded, he wanted her all to himself. For a little while, anyway.

The lights dimmed when he sank into the bed beside her, but Carleen had come prepared. She pulled a miniature flashlight out from underneath the comforter and flipped the switch on. They moved closer together, their shoulders almost touching, so they could both view the photos in the narrow beam of light.

"Wow," he said, focusing on the first picture in her portfolio.

The glossy photograph showed a living room rich with color, unique furniture pieces, and interesting architectural elements. He especially liked the inlaid ceiling and the stained glass panel around the entryway.

"This is one of her favorites," she said, a hint of pride in her voice. "Not a cheap job, by any means, but definitely worth it."

Nate slowly flipped through the pages, impressed by the bland rooms that Mia Maldonado had transformed with a few simple changes. Rooms that came alive under her touch. Much like he was coming alive with Carleen lying so near him. He could smell the scent of gardenias in her hair and wanted to rub his face in the silky strands.

"Here's the bedroom section." She turned another page. "As you can see, there is a wide variety of styles, from rustic country to Victorian—with everything in between."

"So what exactly does Mia have in mind for me?"

She met his gaze and for one insane moment, he thought she was going to kiss him. Then she broke eye contact and turned her attention back to the portfolio.

"She mentioned something about a Tuscan theme, but she'll need your input before a final decision is made. Your house is very minimalist, but is that by design or default?"

He shrugged. "I just buy what I need to get by."

She nodded. "That's what I thought. So, really, the options are wide open. Anything fussy is definitely out. No Victorian or French Provincial. But Tuscan might fit the bill. Or even a Mission style."

"You sound like a decorator."

She closed the book. "Yes, well, I've learned a lot from Mia. But, she's still the expert."

"Since I'm far from an expert, I'm sure I'll be happy with anything she designs."

"I do have one question," she said, snuggling back into her pillow, "though it might be a little personal."

He hesitated, reminding himself that Carleen wasn't stupid. So far, he'd carried out his plan to investigate her without raising any suspicions. But he needed to tread carefully—especially if they became lovers. "What's that?"

"You said the inside of your house is decorated by default. That you haven't put a lot of time or effort into decorating."

"That's true. I'm afraid both decorating and cleaning are at the bottom of my priority list."

"Your house wasn't that messy," she countered. "I've definitely seen worse."

"That's comforting."

She smiled. "You're something of a mystery, Nate. You don't seem to care much about how your house looks on the inside, but the outside is another story. Those rosebushes lining the front of your house are beautiful—and so well tended. Maybe this is sexist, but you just don't strike me as the type of guy to fuss around a flowerbed."

He arched a brow. "So you think flowers are for sissies, huh?"

She closed the portfolio on her lap. "I probably never should have brought up this subject."

"Hey, I'm not offended." He paused, hesitant to reveal too many details of his personal life. This was business, after all. Yet, how could he get her to trust him if he didn't share part of himself? A part that was safe to let go.

"The truth is," he said at last, "those rosebushes are special to me. My grandmother used to live in that house years ago. I remember planting those rosebushes with her when I was six years old. She loved flowers and she loved me. One of the very few people that did."

Carleen turned toward him, her breath a warm caress on his cheek.

He looked into her brown eyes, her face so close to his on the pillow that he could count each one of her thick, dark eyelashes.

"My Gram died when I was eight. The house and all her furnishings were sold at an estate auction. Everything that reminded me of her was gone—except those rosebushes. So when the house came on the market a couple of years ago, I bought it."

She smiled. "That's a beautiful story."

Her gaze held something he couldn't define. Sympathy? Pity? Loss? He'd opened only a small part of his heart to her, but he hated how vulnerable the revelation made him feel. How lonely.

He cupped her cheek, then leaned forward and kissed her. Her lips parted in surprise, allowing his tongue to seek refuge in her warm, sweet mouth. Nate closed his eyes, savoring the taste of her, the feel of her.

Then she kissed him back, filling the void inside of him and sparking the desire he'd fought so long to control. He knew she could feel the pounding of his heart, but he didn't care. All he wanted was to hold her hard against him. To bury himself deep inside her. To forget about everything but the precious sanctuary he saw offered in her eyes.

He deepened the kiss, his hand sliding down her cheek and along the slender column of her throat before finding the heavy weight of her breast. He molded it through the camisole, savoring the way it spilled over his palm.

She moaned when he brushed his thumb over the soft fabric concealing her nipple. Once. Twice. Three times. A perfect pink bud soon formed and he plucked it with his fingertips, drawing more delicious moans of wanton desire from her throat.

Her hands splayed over his shoulders, then trickled over his chest. He wanted her to touch him lower. Much lower. To touch the hard part of him that ached for release and pulsed with the need to feel her hot, sweet tongue on him.

He grasped her hand to show her just what he wanted when the sound of the doorknob turning made him freeze. He broke the kiss as the lights flipped on, rolling back to his side of the bed just as the door opened and Hannah walked inside.

"Sorry to disturb you," she said with a smile, obviously unaware of her ill timing. "There seems to be a malfunction with the bioreadings, so I just wanted to check the machine."

Nate glanced at Carleen, noting the hot flush on her cheeks. "What kind of malfunction?"

"Her heart rate just went off the charts," Hannah said, checking the connections on the jukebox. "The breathing patterns went haywire, too."

Carleen's blush deepened. "Probably just some kind of glitch."

"It does happen occasionally," Hannah said, carefully checking all the cable wires attached to her head. "Everything looks clear from this end."

"That's good to know," Carleen said, refusing to meet Nate's gaze.

Hannah headed toward the door. "Sorry if I woke you. I'll let you two get back to sleep now."

A moment after she'd left the room, the overhead lights switched off again.

"That was a close call," Nate mused.

"What if she saw us?" Carleen asked, an edge of panic in her voice.

"The lights were out," he reminded her. "I doubt she saw anything. Even if she did, I'm almost certain Harlan wouldn't kick us out of the sleep study. He's a romantic at heart."

"It's still too risky." She scooted farther away from Nate on the bed. "We can't let that happen again, Nate. Not here, anyway."

Not here. Those words gave him hope.

The smartest thing he could do was go to sleep

and dream about all the things he wanted to do with her when they were away from the sleep lab. When he was the one in control, not Harlan and his research assistants. How he'd kiss her senseless without worrying about the reading on a biomonitor. How he'd strip off her clothes, piece by piece, so he could look his fill of her glorious body. Then he'd take his time tasting every inch of her. He'd start with each breast, teasing her nipples with his tongue until they were as firm and ripe and sweet as strawberries.

Then he'd move lower, licking his way to the soft, creamy skin of her belly. Then even lower, to the silky nest of curls…

"I think we'd better just go to sleep," she whispered, interrupting his fantasy. "Good night, Nate."

"Good night, Carleen." But sleep was impossible for Nate in his present condition. His body throbbed and his fists clenched, achingly aware that he could make his fantasy come true right now. She was so close. So damn close that he had to bite his tongue to keep from groaning in frustration. Which just proved one thing.

Nate was dangerously out of control.

THE NEXT DAY, Mia walked into her house to find Carleen holding a huge bouquet of white roses.

"Those are gorgeous," Mia said, tossing her purse on a chair. "Toby must really miss you."

"I'm not sure they're from Toby. Or if they're even for me." Carleen placed the flowers in a glass vase on the coffee table, carefully arranging the thorny stems. "They arrived this morning, but with no card attached."

"Who else would send them?"

She shrugged. "Your guess is as good as mine. I asked the florist who delivered them this morning, but he claimed he was sworn to secrecy."

"I'm sure they're from Toby. He probably sent them to make up for that fight you two had when you took him to the airport."

Carleen waved away that possibility. "We settled that ten phone calls ago. I've talked to him every night and he's too wrapped up in his movie to think about placing an order for flowers halfway around the world."

Mia bent down to smell the fragrant blossoms. "They're beautiful, whoever sent them to you."

"I'm not convinced they're for me," Carleen replied. "Maybe Nate sent them."

She straightened at the sound of his name, all the titillating memories from last night coming back in a heated rush. Despite Hannah's untimely interruption, Mia knew now more than ever that making love to Nate was inevitable. A sweet, sensual expectation was building inside of her with each passing day.

"I don't think they're from Nate," Mia said, not allowing herself to even consider that possibility. Right now, she wanted Nate in her bed. If he started romancing her, sending her flowers or love letters, then she'd start wanting more. His love. His heart. His soul. Things she knew instinctively that he couldn't give her.

"Why not?" Carleen countered. "We know he likes

roses. Just look at those beautiful bushes in front of his house. Maybe he's playing secret admirer."

He hadn't kept his admiration secret last night. Just the memory of the skillful way he'd touched her warmed her all the way down to her toes.

"See, you're blushing," Carleen teased. "So it must at least be possible."

In a way, Mia hoped she was right. That would mean Nate didn't hold a grudge for how their night had ended. He'd already been gone this morning when she'd woken up and she hadn't seen or spoken to him since.

Carleen grimaced. "I just thought of another possibility. What about Ian? He threatened to try to win you back, didn't he?"

Mia shrugged. "I wouldn't call it a threat. But he definitely doesn't take rejection well."

"Then it's him," Carleen said. "It has to be."

"I'm not so sure. He never sent me flowers once when we were dating. As I recall, Ian considered them a waste of money because they only last a few days. His idea of romance was buying me tickets to a stock car race."

"I thought you hated stock car races."

"I do," Mia replied. "But Ian loves them. That's why I don't think he sent the flowers. There's nothing in it for him."

Carleen sighed. "I suppose we could stand around here the rest of the afternoon trying to guess who sent them. But we've got work to do. Nate called a little while ago and wants us to meet him at that furniture store on Lexington Avenue."

Her heart jumped at the sound of his name. "He did?"

She nodded. "Isn't that the one with all those cheap imports?"

"One and the same," Mia affirmed. "The place smells like formaldehyde and actually advertises secondhand mattress sets."

"Then let's just hope he hasn't found the second-hand bed of his dreams there."

Mia grabbed her purse and headed for the door, too anxious to see Nate to care why he wanted them there.

"Hold on," Carleen called after. "We have to remember that I'm the decorator here and you're the assistant. Now tell me why I should hate this hypothetical bed that I haven't seen yet."

"Because the bargains you find in Furniture Warehouse aren't worth the money. The craftsmanship is shoddy and I've found their salespeople less than honest about the quality of the components used to construct the furniture."

Mia continued her lesson on furniture all the way to the store. But her heart wasn't really in it. The closer she got to seeing Nate again, the more nervous she became.

"Did Nate want to talk to me when he called?" Mia asked, trying to sound nonchalant.

Carleen hesitated. "Actually…"

Mia knew her friend well enough to recognize that tone and knew it didn't bode well. She pulled into the nearest parking spot and then turned to look at her. "Tell me."

"Don't get mad, but he made a point of asking me to meet him alone."

Her heart dropped. "Why didn't you tell me that back at the house?"

"Because I'm not about to risk dispensing decorating advice on my own. I know nothing about the evils of Furniture Warehouse. You're the expert, remember?"

Disappointment made her voice thick. "But Nate doesn't want me here."

"In the first place, I don't believe that. Did you two have a spat or something?"

"Not exactly."

"In the second place, we need to act like a team if we want to pull this off. That way it's not so obvious who's the decorator and who's the assistant."

As much as Mia hated to admit it, Carleen had a point. Besides, she'd be sleeping with Nate again tonight. Better to get any awkwardness out of the way now.

"All right," Mia said. "Let's do it."

8

THEY FOUND NATE waiting for them in the entrance, looking dark and a little dangerous in faded black jeans and a black T-shirt. Mia couldn't help noticing the flash of surprise on his face when he saw her tagging along.

At least that answered one question—the roses definitely weren't from him.

"Sorry we're late," Carleen said.

"No problem." He led them into the store. "I wasn't expecting both of you to show up."

Ouch. Okay, so the man obviously didn't take rejection well. Which irritated her more than a little, because she had kissed him back last night. Yes, she'd put the brakes on taking that kiss even further, but that didn't give him the right to freeze her out.

Her hurt turned to indignation. *Fine. No problem.* She'd had Nate Cafferty pegged as Mr. Wrong from the start. This just proved her intuition was right.

"I certainly can't complain about sharing the company of two beautiful women. I'll be the envy of every man in this place." Then he smiled at her and all her indignation melted away at the heat she saw in his eyes.

Mia followed Nate and Carleen down a long aisle full of inferior furniture, more confused than ever. First, he didn't want her here and now he'd just called her beautiful. The man had the uncanny ability to twist her heart into a pretzel with just a few words.

Ian might be a jerk, but he was an uncomplicated jerk. She knew he was selfish, deceptive and liked to chase teenage bimbos. Nate was an enigma—and she grew more fascinated with him every day.

But she didn't want to be fascinated. She wanted sex. Simple, uncomplicated sex. With Nate. Was that so much to ask?

"Here it is," Nate said at last. "My dream bed."

Mia stared at the wrought-iron monstrosity in front of her and said one word. "No."

Nate looked at her. "You don't like it?"

"I think it would be perfect if you're planning a Spanish Inquisition theme for your bedroom."

"Hey, don't try to spare my feelings." He grinned. "Tell me how you really feel."

"Okay, that might be a little harsh," she admitted. "But this bed is all wrong for you."

"Maybe we should ask the professional." He turned to Carleen. "Well?"

"It's interesting." Carleen walked around the bed, observing it from all sides. "But I'd say I have to agree with *Carleen*. It doesn't quite fit the design plan I have in mind for your bedroom." Then she froze, her gaze focusing on something across the large warehouse. "Excuse me for a minute. I think I see something…that might work better for you. Stay right here."

Carleen took off down the aisle, leaving the two of them alone.

"I guess the vote is two against one." Nate feigned a mournful look at the bed. "That means you win."

"So do you," she told him. "You'll be much happier with another bed."

He turned all his attention to Mia, taking a step closer to her. "I've learned that it's not the bed that makes you happy, but who's in it with you."

Tension crackled between them and for one crazy moment, she thought he was going to throw her down on the monster bed and finish what he'd started last night. She was almost disappointed when he backed off, digging into his pocket for loose change.

"How about a cup of coffee?" he offered. "My treat."

They walked over to the coffee kiosk and waited in line. The crowd there gave Mia hope that the coffee was of higher quality than the furniture.

"How about your boss?" Nate asked, as they reached the front of the line. "Do you think she'd like a cup?"

The real Mia glanced around the store, but Carleen was nowhere in sight. "Why don't you go ahead and order one for her while I track her down?"

Mia searched the store, walking up and down each aisle. She even checked the restroom. Fifteen minutes later, she met Nate back at the coffee kiosk.

"I can't find her."

Nate handed her a foam cup. "Well, she has to be here somewhere."

Mia took a cautious sip from the steaming cup. "This place is huge. Maybe we just missed each other somehow."

Nate switched the cup holder to his right hand, then looked at his watch. "She's been gone quite a while. Of course, as a decorator, she probably loses all track of time in a place like this."

He was wrong on both counts. Carleen wasn't a decorator and no self-respecting interior designer would spend more than five minutes in the Furniture Warehouse.

"I'm starting to worry," Mia said, as they began to walk the aisles again. "This isn't like, uh, Mia to just disappear for so long."

"Does she have a cell phone with her?" Nate asked, pulling his own from his pocket.

Mia shook her head. "No, she doesn't own one."

What she didn't tell him was that Carleen couldn't afford a cell phone. Toby had offered to buy her one, but Carleen had refused to take anything from him. She was determined to prove to his mother that she didn't want to marry Toby for his money.

Mia admired her principles while doubting they'd have any effect on Mrs. Hamilton's opinion of her son's fiancée.

"Then here's what we'll do," Nate said. "I'll search the store again while you have one of the clerks announce her name over the intercom."

"Good idea."

They parted company, heading off in opposite directions. Mia liked Nate's take-charge attitude, though nothing could stop the seed of worry growing inside of her. It wasn't like Carleen to just disappear like this.

Then another thought occurred to her. What if she'd done it to give Nate and Mia time alone? Perhaps she'd sensed the initial tension between them. It was a possibility, but there was no way that Mia could know for certain.

She finally found a clerk and spilled a disjointed story about losing "Mia." At first, the clerk thought she was talking about a child and wanted to put the store's abduction policy into full gear. When Mia finally straightened him out, he seemed to resent her wanting to use the intercom system to find a lost friend.

"Can't you just make a call to her cell phone?" he asked.

"She doesn't have one."

He shook his head. "Who doesn't have a cell phone these days?" The man flipped on the intercom system, then picked up the microphone. "Okay, what's her name?"

"Carleen Wimmer." The name was barely off her lips before she realized her mistake. "No, wait, her name is—"

"Carleen Wimmer," the store clerk announced over the speaker system. "Please come to the front of the store. *Carleen Wimmer,* your friends are looking for you."

"Her name is Mia Maldonado," she said with a groan, realizing it was too late.

The clerk scowled at her. "Is this some kind of joke? Because I have customers, lady, so you'll have to get your jollies somewhere else."

He stalked off before she had a chance to explain. Not that her explanation would make much sense. But she needed to come up with something halfway reasonable to say to Nate.

By the time she found him, she had an excuse ready. "I think that clerk was confused. I gave him my name and told him we were looking for Mia. He must have mixed them up."

"It doesn't matter. She left a note on my windshield. I saw it when I went out to check the parking lot."

"What?" Mia exclaimed as Nate pulled a slip of paper from his shirt pocket.

He handed to her. "You don't have to worry. She's fine."

"'Just remembered an appointment I have with my hairdresser today,'" Mia read the hasty scribblings aloud. "'If you're a no-show, he drops you as a client, so I've gotta run! Sorry to bail on you. Mia.'"

"I have to say Mia's customer service is a little unusual. Does she usually abandon her clients in furniture stores?"

The real Mia shook her head. "She's never done anything like this before."

Something told her this wasn't the real reason for Carleen's vanishing act. It probably had to do with the wedding and she was covering so Nate wouldn't suspect anything.

At least Mia knew she was all right.

Then she looked up and saw Nate staring at her in a way that made her knees turn to jelly. He took a step closer to her, heat flashing in his eyes.

"You know what this means, don't you?"

She licked her dry lips. "What?"

"I get to take you home."

IT WAS the longest drive of her life.

Mia sat in the passenger seat of Nate's sports car, watching his hand work the stick shift. Each time he switched gears, the motor gunned and she could feel the vibrations rumbling the seat beneath her. Anticipation pulsed in the very core of her, fueled by the sight of his broad fingers wrapped around the shift knob situated between them.

Those same fingers had caressed her breast last night, promising even more pleasures—until they'd been interrupted. Now there was nothing in their way. No biomonitors. No tangle of cable wires. No lab assistant to spoil the moment.

Mia saw the empty driveway when Nate turned onto her street and knew that Carleen hadn't come home yet. Which meant the house was empty as well.

A carnal awareness thrummed between them, so when he pulled into the driveway and cut the engine, neither one of them moved or said a word. They hadn't spoken since they'd left the store. Each knew exactly what this moment portended. They didn't need to talk about it or discuss the ramifications. They were both past the point of verbalizing what they wanted.

Mia knew this was the point of no return. Despite her past mistakes, she decided to leap into the abyss without weighing any of the consequences. Turning to face him, she rasped, "Do you want to come inside?"

Heat flared in his green eyes and Nate gave a sharp nod.

They barely made it through the front door when he pulled her roughly into his arms and kissed her hard and deep. She kicked the door closed, then reached blindly behind her to lock it.

The weight of his body propelled her against the door as he deepened the kiss, his hips grinding against her. She met him measure for measure, her tongue battling his for control as the heat built between them.

She tore at his shirt, buttons popping and bouncing on the Mexican tile. Fabric ripped and Mia broke their kiss, then lowered her head to slash her tongue across his chest.

He dropped his head back and groaned low in his throat, his hard arousal throbbing against her belly. She sank to her knees, fumbling with the button fly at his waist, then pulling his slacks down over his hips.

The virile scent of musk and man assailed her nostrils and she reached out to cup him over his boxer shorts. The contact drew a hoarse cry from his throat and he yanked her up, kissing her again as his hands moved beneath her blouse.

Mia closed her eyes, letting herself drift in the flurry of exquisite sensations. His rough hands on her breasts. His mouth following, wet and wicked. The cool air hitting her bare bottom when he pulled her skirt and panties off.

Then he lay down on the tile floor, pulling her on top of him. They were both naked now, though she had no memory of how it had happened. She was too caught up in the moment, aware only of giving and taking pleasure. Savoring every moan that escaped his lips and the erotic words he whispered in her ear. He surpassed all her fantasies, taking her to a place of primal, sexual need that she'd never been before. A place that made her do and say things she'd never imagined.

She touched him…everywhere. Tasted him…everywhere. Until Nate pulled her on top of him and held her there, his breath coming in deep gasps as he visibly fought for control.

Mia had never felt so desired. So sexy. She kissed him, savoring the way he moaned deep in his throat as her body molded to him.

"Do you want to come inside?" she said huskily, repeating her earlier invitation. Only this one had an entirely different meaning.

Nate didn't have to be asked twice. He lifted her hips, positioning her above his erect shaft. He already wore a condom—another mystery in the haze of desire that enveloped her. She had no concept of time or place or purpose. Only this precise moment mattered, when she took him deep inside of her, inch by precious inch, until he filled her body, mind and soul.

Nate sucked in a deep breath, too overcome to move. She was so hot and slick and wet. So perfect for him. He didn't want this moment to end.

But his body had a will of its own, rising off the floor in a timeless rhythm that promised sweet release all too soon. She moved with him, her hands clenched on his shoulders, her hair trickling over his face.

As her breathing quickened, Nate looked into her

face and commanded her to open her eyes. He wanted to watch her pleasure. To see her come apart on top of him.

It didn't take long.

One thrust. Two. Then a cry of satisfaction ripped from her throat and her eyelids drooped as she writhed on top of him. Her inner spasms snapped the little control he had left. He grasped her hips, pressing her tightly against him until his world exploded.

A world that would never be the same for him again.

MIA LAY IN HER BED, wrapped in Nate's arms, when she heard the front door open. She lifted her head off the pillow and squinted at the clock on her nightstand.

It was almost six o'clock. Only four more hours until they were due at the sleep lab. Carefully extricating herself from Nate's embrace, she slipped out of bed and reached for her clothes.

"Just like a woman," Nate teased in a voice still rough with sleep. "You get what you want, then you just try to sneak away."

"I was trying not to wake you," she replied, leaning down to kiss his cheek. "And as I remember, we both got what we wanted—twice."

He grinned. "That's right. No wonder I can't move."

"Then stay in bed," she suggested. "I think I heard Mia come home and I just want to make sure she's all right."

"I don't want to stay here without you," he said, slowly rising to his feet in all his naked magnificence.

Mia took a moment to savor the vision, then began

to dress, her limbs heavy with the torpor of sexual satisfaction.

They descended the stairs several minutes later, exchanging glances as they reached the tile foyer. Mia knew she'd never walk through her front door again without picturing Nate lying there naked and fully aroused, reaching out to pull her down on top of him.

She smiled. "Thank you for bringing me home."

He grasped one of her hands in his and gave it a gentle squeeze. "Believe me, it was my pleasure."

The innocent gesture touched her more than the hours of unbridled sex they'd just enjoyed. She struggled for something nonchalant to say, but made the mistake of looking into his face and losing herself in his green eyes.

The sound of water running in the kitchen brought her to her senses. "Sounds like someone is fixing supper."

"Talk about perfect timing," Nate said, following her down the hallway. "I'm starving."

They found her roommate standing at the kitchen sink, making a pitcher of iced tea.

"Your hair looks exactly the same to me," Mia said, taking a seat at the table. "I hope your hairdresser didn't charge you too much for it."

"Actually," Carleen turned off the faucet, "I ended up missing the appointment, so all it cost me was a new hairdresser."

"That's too bad," Mia commiserated. "Though I have to admit you had me worried when you just disappeared like that at the Furniture Warehouse."

"I'm so sorry." Carleen placed the pitcher in the refrigerator. "I know it was rude of me to just take off like that. I guess I just panicked when I realized I forgot about that appointment."

Mia walked over to the sink and placed her palm on Carleen's forehead. "Are you sure you feel all right? You look a little pale."

"I'm fine," she assured her. "It's nothing, really. Probably just a small panic attack now that the wedding is almost here."

Nate's brow crinkled in confusion. "You're having panic attacks about Carleen's wedding?"

The real Carleen's eyes widened at her error, but Mia laughed to cover the gaffe. "She's been doing all the worrying for me. Mia's somewhat of a perfectionist while I tend to let the small details slide."

The longer Mia knew Nate, the more she hated lying to him. Especially now that they'd been intimate. But she was in too deep to back out now. The sleep study would be over in just over two weeks and if she confessed her masquerade, Nate might feel honor-bound to tell his foster father the truth.

She simply couldn't afford to risk it.

"I've always been a worrier," Carleen told him, recovering nicely. "And I'm still fighting off this flu bug that seems to have zapped me. I guess I need to start eating right and taking better care of myself."

"Then you can start right now," Mia said. "I'll fix dinner tonight."

"And I'll help," Nate chimed in and then turned to Mia. "If you don't mind an extra mouth to feed."

Since she had a special fondness for his mouth, she didn't mind at all. "We'd love to have you join us."

"Hold on a minute," Carleen interjected. "Don't you two have to leave for the Longo estate soon?"

Nate checked his watch. "Not for another couple of hours or so. Plenty of time to whip up something."

"I really am perfectly fine," Carleen insisted.

"You still have to eat," Mia propelled her toward the kitchen door. "Now go lie down upstairs until I call for you."

Carleen knew better than to argue when Mia was in one of her take-charge moods. After she left, Mia did a quick mental inventory of the refrigerator. Her usual fare of tuna salad on rye probably wouldn't impress Nate. And Carleen needed something more substantial in her stomach.

"What sounds good to you?" she asked as Nate followed her into the kitchen.

"This," he said huskily, coming up behind her and nibbling the back of her neck. His arms wrapped around the front of her waist, then he pulled her back against his chest.

She closed her eyes as his lips moved to the curve of her shoulder. They'd made love twice, but something told her she'd never get enough of Nate. His hands splayed over her hips, pressing her buttocks against his groin.

"You taste wonderful," he whispered against her cheek. "I think I'll have you for dinner."

She turned in his arms, heat pooling low in her body. "How about dessert?"

He leaned closer to her mouth. "I don't think I can wait that long."

But before he could kiss her, the doorbell rang.

Mia leaned her head against Nate's chest and swallowed a sigh. "I'd better get that."

"We could ignore it," he suggested, his hands sliding up to her waist.

"I know, but Mia won't and she needs her rest."

Nate kissed the top of her head, then let her go. "All right. But I'm holding you to that dessert offer."

She smiled. "We'd better eat dinner first. How about spaghetti?"

He nodded. "I'll start the water boiling while you answer the door."

"There's a pot in the cupboard next to the dishwasher," she told him, moving toward the living room. "I'll be right back."

When Mia reached the front door, she smoothed her hair then opened it. Ian Brock stood on the other side.

"Surprise," he said, his arms full of boxes from his favorite Chinese restaurant.

"What are you doing here?"

He walked past her and into the dining room, setting the boxes on the table. "I'm here to talk about our business proposition. Since I know how much you like Chinese, I thought I'd surprise you."

"Thanks, but I have company."

Nate chose that moment to walk through the kitchen door, a cotton dish towel slung over one broad shoulder. "The water is on the stove. What else can I do?"

His appearance startled Ian for a moment, but he recovered quickly. "Hello, I'm Ian Brock."

Nate hesitated a moment, then reached out and shook his hand, casting a curious glance at Mia. "Nate Cafferty."

"Ian used to work here," she explained.

Ian smiled. "Among other things."

She watched Ian begin to unload the sacks, placing chopsticks and packets of sweet and sour sauce on the table. She could feel the undercurrent of testosterone in the air and it was obvious no matter what she said Ian wasn't going anywhere.

Panic set in when Mia realized how easily Ian could destroy everything. All he had to do was say her name to set disaster in motion. Which only left her with one, horrible alternative.

"I'm sorry, Nate," she said, not able to meet his eyes. "I'm going to have to give you a raincheck on dinner. Ian and I need to talk business."

It took a moment for her words to sink in. "Oh. Okay."

Banishing Nate was the last thing she wanted to do, but what choice did she have? She wanted nothing more than to kick Ian, along with his smug grin, out of her house. But she knew he'd put up a fight—and possibly blurt out her real name—so she simply couldn't risk it.

"But I'll see you tonight," she promised, trying to widen the distance between the two men as quickly as possible.

Nate stood in the doorway, looking completely confused. "Yeah, sure. Whatever."

"Thanks again for…everything."

"No problem." He pulled the dish towel off his shoulder and handed it to her. Then he turned and walked out of the house without another word.

Mia stared after him, hating what had just happened. But what could she do? Ian was still in the house. She'd have to wait and apologize to Nate tonight in bed. Find some way to make him understand.

"Dinner is served," Ian said behind her.

She closed the door and turned around, her appetite completely ruined. "I'm not hungry."

"I brought your favorite," Ian said, holding up a paper box and a pair of chopsticks, trying to entice her. "Cashew chicken."

She folded her arms across her chest. "My favorite is almond chicken. Now I want you to leave."

He set down the box and the chopsticks, then slowly advanced on her. "I think you don't know what you want, Mia."

She gritted her teeth, but neither her body language nor her expression seemed to deter him.

Ian grasped her shoulders, looking intently into her eyes. "Can't you feel this electricity between us? It's there. You know it's there."

"The only thing I know is that you barged in here without an invitation. The only reason you want me back is because you think another man wants me. Well, get this, Ian. I don't want you."

"Prove it," he said, then pulled her to him for a kiss.

His lips pressed hard against hers, his tongue angling for entrance. She stood motionless for a moment, too stunned to move. He mistook her stillness for compliance, yanking her closer to him.

She recoiled, pushing firmly against his chest until he broke the kiss.

"Consider that an appetizer," he said, slightly breathless, his hands still on her shoulders.

She twisted away from him and marched toward the door. "Out."

He placed his hands on his hips. "I'm not going anywhere until you settle down so we can have a rational discussion."

"Fine," she said, reaching over to grab her purse off the chair. "Then *I'll* leave."

He started after her. "Where are you going?"

"That's none of your business, but don't bother sticking around here, because I won't be back tonight."

His mouth thinned. "Does that mean you're spending the night with Nate again?"

"Ian, let's get one thing clear," Mia said, struggling to keep her voice calm. "You and I are history, which means I don't have to tell you where I'm going or whom I see."

"I could follow you," he threatened.

"And I could call the police and report you as a stalker."

He shook his head. "You're making a big mistake. I'm in love with you, Mia. I care about you. I don't want a man like Nate Cafferty breaking your heart."

"I can take care of myself," she assured him.

The telephone rang, but she ignored it.

"Do you want me to get it?" Ian asked on the third ring.

"No, let the machine pick it up."

He moved back into the dining room. "Look, I won't try to stop you or follow you. If you want to run after Nate, that's your choice. At least take the Cashew chicken. I bought it for you."

"I lost my appetite. Give it to Carleen."

The telephone stopped ringing and the answering machine switched on. Carleen's voice cheerfully asked the caller to leave a message. For a moment, there was silence; then Elvis began to sing "Love Me Tender."

"Does Elvis call here often?" Ian quipped, looking at the answering machine.

Mia rushed over and picked up the receiver. "Hello? Who's there?"

But Elvis just kept singing. She listened until the end of the song. Then the dial tone sounded in her ear.

"So who was it?" Ian asked.

She shook her head. "I don't know."

"Carleen's a big Elvis fan, isn't she?" Ian said. "Maybe it was for her."

Or maybe it was Nate, trying to send her some kind of message. First with the bouquet of roses, which she knew held special meaning for him. Then the Elvis song, which he thought held special meaning for her.

But anonymity didn't seem like Nate's style. Why would he hide behind a bouquet of flowers and Elvis?

"You look a little spooked," Ian observed. "Are you sure you still want to go out tonight?"

"I'm positive." She owed Nate an apology and some kind of explanation before he concluded the worst about her.

"Shall I wait here for you?"

She swallowed a groan of frustration, wondering how long it would take for him to get the message. Ian's kiss had proved to her that she no longer harbored any romantic feelings for him whatsoever.

"No," she said as gently as she could under the circumstances. "It's over between us, Ian. Please deal with it and have a nice life."

She brushed past him to turn off the pot that was on the boil and then tell Carleen where she was going.

Then she walked out the door.

9

SOME MEN MIGHT BE put off by a little competition, but Nate Cafferty wasn't one of them. Prowling the Elvis suite that night, he was ready to convince Carleen that she didn't want Ian Brock or Tobias Hamilton.

That the only man she wanted was him.

Because he sure as hell wanted her. That fact had hit him like a brick the moment he'd seen Ian Brock with her tonight. Jealousy had risen up inside of him, threatening to boil over. His first instinct had been to put his fist through the guy's smart mouth.

Instead, he reined in those emotions, using them to focus on the prize, just like he'd been taught by his old boxing coach. As a teenager, the prize had been a championship belt or cold, hard cash.

Now the prize was Carleen.

He knew going into this assignment that she was no ordinary woman. It's true that his pride had taken a serious blow when she'd chosen Ian over him tonight, but once he'd let his temper cool he'd remembered his earlier suspicions that the man was blackmailing her.

The more he thought about it, the more sense it made. She certainly hadn't seemed happy to see him tonight. In fact, she'd practically pushed Nate out the door in a panic to get rid of him. The only reasonable explanation for her behavior was that Ian Brock might say something that she didn't want Nate to hear.

Which brought him full circle to his original problem. She still didn't trust him, even after experiencing the greatest form of intimacy two people could share. But he wasn't about to give up yet.

She might have dined with Ian this evening, but tonight and every night for the next seventeen days, she'd be sleeping with Nate.

Carleen arrived in the Elvis suite even earlier than expected, though Nate was already in bed. Even after their marathon lovemaking session this afternoon, his body tensed at the sight of her, kicking his libido into high gear.

Her eyes widened in surprise at the sight of him. "I didn't think you'd be here yet."

"Looks like we're both early tonight. What happened to your dinner date?"

"It wasn't a date," she clarified. "I didn't even know Ian was coming over."

Yet, she'd shown Nate the door the moment her old boyfriend had arrived. Jealousy flared again, but he tamped it down, sucking in a deep breath. "I'm just glad you're here."

"I have a busy day tomorrow," she replied, heading toward the bathroom, duffel bag in hand. "I wanted to get a good night's sleep."

"Not tonight, Carleen," he murmured under his breath, as she disappeared into Graceland. "Not tonight."

When she emerged several minutes later, Nate closed his eyes and feigned sleep. The mattress dipped with her weight as she climbed into bed beside him.

Her warmth seeped over to his side of the bed and his body hardened at the thought of how easy it would be to reach over and touch her. To run his fingers over the curve of her hip and along the supple line of her buttocks.

Several minutes passed as the fantasy took full flight. A fantasy that went way beyond solving this case or fulfilling his lust. He wanted Carleen naked in his arms again.

"Nate?" she whispered softly.

"Yes," he replied, opening his eyes. Her dark hair gleamed in the neon glow of the jukebox and she'd never looked so lovely.

"I'm just wondering why Hannah hasn't come in to hook me up to the jukebox yet."

"It's too early," he explained. "Just after nine o'clock. She won't hook you up until ten so the readings can be as consistent as possible."

"Oh." Carleen sighed. "I thought maybe she forgot about me."

"I don't see how anyone could forget about you."

Her lips parted in surprise, then curved into a smile. "So you're not mad at me anymore?"

He blinked in surprise. "For what?"

"For what happened this evening when Ian arrived at my house. I'm usually not that rude, I was just a little…stressed."

He reached out to sweep an errant curl off her

cheek, relishing the silky feel of her face beneath his fingertips. "Maybe I can help."

Her brow furrowed. "How?"

"Do you trust me?"

She hesitated, the pink tip of her tongue darting out to moisten her lips. "Yes, Nate. I trust you."

He released a breath he didn't know he'd been holding. Now that he'd won her trust, he was determined to keep it. He'd let her set the pace. Let her stop him the moment she said the word, even if it killed him.

Then he reached out and touched her.

10

MIA'S BREATH caught in her throat when she felt the touch of Nate's fingers on her hand. Gentle. Featherlight. Then he began stroking up and down her arm, over and over again, and taut nerves in her body began to unfurl.

She dropped her gaze, watching his fingers move up and down. Yet with each journey, they climbed a little higher. When they reached the top of her shoulder, his fingers brushed over her collarbone, skimming the top of her camisole.

She met his gaze, knowing she should protest, but the words died on her lips. The truth was that she didn't want him to stop. Not now. Not ever.

Nate leaned in close, his mouth near her own, his fingers still moving. They touched the base of her throat, where her pulse fluttered wildly. A smile lifted the corners of his lips, and then his hand slid over her shoulder and down her arm again, lingering at the tender skin on the inside of her wrist.

He seemed to have an innate sense of how to arouse her with the lightest brush of his fingertips. Just like this afternoon. Just like he was doing now, innocently stroking her arm.

Or maybe not so innocently.

It startled her to realize how vulnerable she felt at this moment. How being tethered to the jukebox had been almost a kind of security device for her. Now it was just she and Nate, alone in the Elvis suite, without any machine to record her physical reaction to him. A good thing, too, since her heart was racing in her chest and she had trouble catching her breath.

The fact that Hannah or Harlan or any of the lab personnel could walk in at any moment only seemed to heighten the erotic sensations swirling around inside of her. Yes, it was risky. But she couldn't reject Nate now. Not after what had happened with Ian earlier this evening.

And not when she knew where this would lead.

Nate's touch rendered her incapable of rational thought. Of weighing the risks against the rewards. Because the reward his fingertips promised drove every other notion from her head.

His hand moved higher, this time slipping beneath the thin strap of her camisole and brushing so close to her breast that she thought she'd imagined it. Until he did it again.

Mia gasped aloud at the exquisite sensation and when his fingers closed over her breast, she arched up to meet his touch. She wrapped her fingers in his hair, savoring the weight of his body against her.

Nate leaned closer, pressing his lips against the tender skin of her throat. His hands gently cupped her breasts, plucking her nipples through the silky fabric.

She wanted more. Desire pounded in her veins,

echoing the hot throb deep in her groin. She knew he was holding back. Sensed his restraint. Feared he'd stop too soon.

She needed to be close to him. To assuage the desperate throbbing ache between her thighs and the empty ache in her heart.

He shifted slightly, lying back on the bed, then pulling her on top of him. She settled into his body, his erection deliciously positioned between her thighs. She moved against him, drawing a groan from deep in his chest.

Then his hands slid down her back and beneath the elastic waistband of her pajama pants. They cupped her bare buttocks, then pressed her against him. They both moaned softly at the sensation before Nate captured her mouth once more.

As he kissed her, his fingers moved lower, until they found the secret spot that made her cry out.

"Oh, yes. Right there."

Nate heeded her pleas, his fingers working magic between her thighs until Mia couldn't speak at all. Couldn't do anything but rock against him, seeking sweet relief from the delicious ache building inside of her.

His fingers never stopped moving, playing her like a violin. They strummed her delicate flesh until it swelled beneath his touch.

The beat of desire kept building inside of her until she lost track of time and place. She hovered over him, her eyes closed. From somewhere far off she could hear him gently urging her to let go.

Then the crescendo came crashing upon her unexpectedly and she arched up in surprise. Her body shuddered, his mouth catching her cries of release. Then he wrapped his arms around her, holding her against him as the waves rippled through her.

Mia lay atop him, shocked by what had just happened, but too overcome by the experience to move. Nate still held her, his body rock-hard under her own. She'd never experienced anything like that while still wearing her clothes. His touch had completely undone her.

"Carleen," he whispered, cupping her cheek with his hand. "I need—"

But before he could tell her what he needed, the door creaked open and the overhead light automatically switched on.

"Good evening," Hannah said, as she backed into the room, pulling a small cart with her through the door.

Mia leapt off Nate and resumed lying on her side of the bed, pulling the comforter up to her neck before Hannah turned around and saw her.

"Good evening," Mia said, her voice shaky to her own ears.

The lab assistant pushed the cart up to the juke-box. "We're having some problems with a few of the monitors, so I'm performing some simple tests on each unit before we hook you up for the night."

"Great," Nate said, sounding less than enthusiastic.

Mia lay beside him in the bed as Hannah methodically tested each connection, her body still thrumming with the aftereffects of Nate's sexual skill.

"Are you all right?" Hannah asked, as she hooked

the first cable wire to Mia's forehead. "You look a little flushed."

"I'm fine," she lied, lying perfectly still and trying
to breathe steadily. "Perfectly fine."

Nate didn't say anything, but she could feel his
gaze on her.

"There you go," Hannah said as she attached the
last lead to her forehead. "Now you're all set."

Neither one of them said a word until Hannah left
the room. As the door closed behind her, the bright
overhead light switched off once more.

"Alone at last," Nate said, leaning up on one
elbow to look down at her.

She licked her lips, wondering what the proper
etiquette was when a man had just given you the
best orgasm of your life. "Thank you" didn't seem
adequate.

"I don't know what to say."

He smiled. "Then don't say anything. Just let me
hold you."

"But you didn't—"

Nate stopped her words with a kiss. "That's right.
Just watching you gives me pleasure."

She arched a brow. "So you don't want to..."

"Oh, I definitely want to," he said huskily. "More
than you'll ever know. But all those cables attached
to your head make it a little difficult."

"Not to mention unattractive," she mused.

He looked deep into her eyes. "If you only knew
how much I want you right now. But I don't want us
to be interrupted again. So I'm willing to wait until
I can find the perfect moment." He caressed her

cheek with his palm. "The perfect moment to make love to you again."

Then he kissed her. A kiss full of desire and heat and anticipation. A kiss that ended much too soon.

"Goodnight, Carleen," Nate whispered, cradling her in his arms."

Mia lay in his embrace, her mind whirling. She'd just been brought to climax again by a man who didn't even know her real name. The situation was spinning out of control. But she wasn't sure she ever wanted it to stop.

THE NEXT MORNING, Mia awoke as Hannah was removing the last electrode from her forehead.

"Good morning," Hannah whispered. "Sorry I woke you."

"That's all right," Mia replied, aware of Nate's soft, steady breathing beside her. He'd moved to his side of the bed sometime during the night, though she'd fallen asleep in his arms.

When Hannah was finished, she waved goodbye and then tiptoed out of the room. The overhead light flashed on as the door opened, then off again as it closed, but neither the movement nor the light woke the man beside her.

Mia turned on her side to watch him, content in this rare opportunity to study Nate unaware. His dark lashes matched the thick stubble over his cheeks and jaw. His nose had a little bump in the middle that looked out of place, making her wonder if he'd broken it sometime in the past.

She knew that Harlan had been his foster father

and that Nate had joined the Longo family as a teenager, but he'd never shared the reason why. Other than his grandmother and the rose bushes, she knew nothing about his past. When she'd cleared his bedroom for the painters, Mia hadn't seen any family photographs anywhere in the house. In fact, it was strangely sparse of any personal keepsakes. Nothing that told her what kind of man he was outside the sleep lab.

Nate fascinated her. Tempted her. Maybe for the simple reason that he was somewhat of a mystery. Perhaps he felt the same way about her. Maybe the passion they shared was fueled by the unknown. Two virtual strangers coming together for a few nights of elicit passion and then parting, perhaps never to see each other again.

That thought produced a curious pang of disappointment inside of her. Harlan's experiment might not be over, but it had proven to her that sleeping with someone every night does affect the way you feel about them.

And she'd realized that even before Nate had touched her last night.

That's how *she* felt, anyway. Mia had no way of knowing if Nate felt the same. Last night might have been nothing more than simple sexual pleasure to him. He'd made no promises to her—other than wanting to continue where they'd left off last night.

And wasn't that all she wanted? One last fling before she found a man who could provide her with a stable home and family, if not the wild sexual satisfaction she'd experienced last night?

Mia wasn't so sure anymore. She climbed quietly out of bed, not wanting him to wake and find her mooning over him. Not only would it make both of them uncomfortable, but she wasn't prepared to hear him say that he wasn't ready for a serious relationship. At least, not until she was fully armored behind clothes and makeup.

But upon emerging from the Graceland bathroom ten minutes later to find him still asleep, Mia took the coward's way out and grabbed her duffel bag before heading for the door.

Harlan stood inside the hub with all his lab assistants, greeting her with a wide smile when he saw her appear. "You're up bright and early this morning, Carleen. How did you sleep?"

"Just fine," she replied, sparing him the details.

"Wonderful," he exclaimed. "I couldn't be happier with your participation in my study. We're receiving some fascinating results."

So had she. This sleep study had helped her put Ian in the past where he belonged, given her a new appreciation for Elvis and introduced her to a man she'd never forget. And it would all end in exactly sixteen days.

As Mia left the Longo estate, the gorgeous autumn morning lifted her flagging spirits. The rising sun peeked through the trees in the east and a trio of ducklings splashed and squawked in the moat. The scent of pine lingered in the air as she made the long trek back to her car.

Maybe she and Nate could spend some time together after the sleep study was over. She'd have to tell him the truth about her identity, of course, and hope that he'd forgive her for deceiving him. A risk, in her estimation, but she had no desire to keep living the lie that she was Carleen.

Or to profit from the lie. As soon as her income improved, she planned to start repaying Harlan Longo every penny of the stipend, with interest. She liked the man too much to take his money under the circumstances.

She passed the abandoned school bus, one of the chickens standing near the open doorway, watching her. Mia couldn't quite understand Longo's fondness for the birds, a messy breed judging by the state of the grounds.

Her own life was a mess, but that would change soon. Thanks to the radio advertisements, her client list was slowly increasing. Her money situation would stabilize eventually, even if going into business with Ian wasn't feasible now. While the plan was solid, it was clear to her that she didn't need or want Ian in her life—in any capacity.

She did, however, want Nate. A flush of anticipation shot through her body when she remembered his promise to find the perfect moment to make love to her again.

A promise that she hoped he intended to keep very soon.

11

WHEN MIA ARRIVED home, she began to have second thoughts about leaving the Elvis suite so abruptly this morning. What would Nate think when he woke up to find her gone? But before she could analyze the situation from every conceivable angle—as she was prone to do in all her relationships—the doorbell rang.

Her first thought was that Nate had come after her, but a quick peek out the window put an end to that possibility. A stranger stood on her front stoop. He was a stocky man, dressed in a dated gray suit and tie.

She checked her watch as she walked to the front door, noting that it was just past eight o'clock in the morning. She hadn't wanted to wake Carleen, hoping the extra sleep would do her some good.

When she opened the door, Mia was surprised to find the man, who had looked older through the window, actually appeared to be in his early thirties. He stood only a couple of inches taller than Mia's five foot six, and wore a pair of silver wire-rimmed glasses.

He blinked at her behind a pair of thick lenses, then smiled. "You must be Ms. Maldonado."

"Yes, I am."

"I'm Sam Kowalski and I've heard wonderful things about your decorating abilities. In fact, I'd like to talk to you about redecorating my game room."

"Right now?" she asked, not remembering his name on her appointment calendar.

"Is this a bad time? I was just on my way into work and I thought I'd stop by to see if you were interested in the job. If you'd like me to schedule another time—"

"No," she interjected, opening the door wider. "That's not necessary. Please come in."

"Thank you." He walked inside, his gaze wandering slowly around the room. "Are we alone?"

Something about the way he asked the question made her uncomfortable, though he looked harmless enough. "Actually, my office assistant is right upstairs. Why?"

"Oh, I just don't want to intrude if you're busy. I really should have called first. I'm afraid I'm rather impulsive that way."

"I can be that way myself sometimes," she assured him, motioning for Mr. Kowalski to have a seat. "My first appointment isn't for another hour."

"Wonderful." He placed his briefcase beside the wing chair, then sat down. "I must say you have a great place here."

"Thank you." She picked up a pen and notepad off the desk. "Now tell me about this game room."

"Well, it's not officially a game room yet," he said. "Right now, it's just a big empty room in my basement. But I'd like to turn it into a game room and I thought I should hire a professional to help me do it." His gaze flicked up and down her body. "That the professional happens to be a beautiful woman is a definite bonus."

Mia forced a smile, telling herself that she was in no position to be picky about her clients. That didn't mean she couldn't set him straight about how she conducted business. "Thank you for the compliment, Mr. Kowalski, but it's unnecessary and makes me a little uncomfortable. In fact, I'd prefer that we keep our relationship purely professional."

"That's fine," he replied, holding up both hands. "I certainly meant no offense."

"None taken," she told him. "Now, let's talk some more about this game room you want me to design for you."

Thirty minutes later, Mia had heard everything she wanted to know about Mr. Kowalski's love for table tennis, billiards, darts and beers of the world. He seemed to revel in the sound of his own voice, yet he still hadn't given any specific details about how he'd like his basement room decorated.

"How about a sports bar theme?" she suggested, trying to steer the conversation into a more productive direction. "Then you could highlight your beer can collection. We could put a bar in one corner of the room and still have plenty of space for the billiard table."

He shrugged, looking less than enthused. "That's a possibility, but I was hoping for something a bit more original. Why don't you draw up a few different plans and I'll stop by later today and pick them up?"

She forced another smile, already certain this client was going to be trouble. Mia had seen his type before. He'd make her draw up multiple plans, finding fault with each one, until she was ready to pay *him* to make a decision.

"I won't have time to do them today," she told him. "But if you'd like to leave a retainer, I could have some preliminary plans drawn up by the end of the week."

He hesitated. "How much money are we talking about here?"

"My standard retainer for this kind of project is three hundred dollars."

He shrugged. "I guess I can bring you a check this afternoon. Will you be around?"

"If I'm not, my assistant can take care of it."

"Perfect." He rose to his feet and then held out his hand. "It's been a pleasure, Ms. Maldonado."

"Please call me Mia," she said, shaking his hand.

"Mia." He smiled, holding her hand a moment longer than necessary before releasing his grasp.

She watched him walk out the door, half hoping he'd change his mind about hiring her so that she'd never have to see him again. Then again, enduring a client like Mr. Kowalski was preferable to bankruptcy.

Mia spent the next hour browsing the latest art catalog, looking for the perfect print for Nate's bedroom. They still hadn't selected a bed, but the room was coming together nicely.

He'd be ready to move back into his bedroom in about two weeks—coinciding with the end of the sleep study.

When the clock chimed, she looked up, surprised to see it was almost eleven o'clock. Concerned that Carleen hadn't emerged from her room yet, she walked to the base of the stairs.

"Carleen?"

There was no answer, making Mia wish she'd have checked on her earlier, especially since Carleen hadn't been feeling well lately.

When she reached Carleen's room, she tilted her head toward the closed door to listen for any sign of movement inside, hating to wake her if she was asleep. Then she tapped lightly on the door. "Carleen?"

Still no answer. She placed her hand on the door-knob and slowly opened the door. The room was empty, the bed neatly made, almost as if it hadn't been slept in.

Carleen had disappeared without a word. Again.

"Maybe Tobias came home early," she muttered to herself, trying to rationalize her friend's increasingly odd behavior.

But even that didn't explain why she'd take off without a word. Carleen Wimmer was one of the most responsible people Mia had ever known. Stress or no stress, flu or no flu, she simply didn't abdicate her office duties, or leave her best friend stranded in a furniture store, or imagine that someone was following her.

As Mia walked back downstairs, she had the awful feeling that something was seriously wrong. She picked up the telephone and dialed Tobias Hamilton's condo. Even if he wasn't back from Frankfurt yet, she knew that Carleen had a key. Maybe she'd gone over there to water his plants.

The phone rang five times before the answering machine clicked on. Mia hung up the phone before the beep. Carleen either wasn't there or she wasn't answering.

Worry continued to nibble at her. In the year they'd lived together, Carleen had never just vanished. This week, she'd done it twice. It was time to find out what was really going on.

So when Carleen walked through the front door an hour later, Mia confronted her.

"Where have you been?"

Carleen winced at her tone. "I'm sorry, Mia. I got a call from the caterer early this morning about some last-minute changes to the reception menu. I never thought I'd be gone so long."

Her explanation sounded perfectly reasonable—but Mia wasn't buying it. "Carleen, I know something is wrong. You haven't been yourself for weeks. Please tell me. I want to help."

Carleen turned away from her. "I know I've been a basket case lately. Please just bear with me a little while longer. Once Toby and I are married, everything will be all right."

"This is about more than wedding stress," Mia insisted. "What are you keeping from me? Please just tell me what's going on."

"I can't," Carleen replied, twisting her hands together. "Look, please don't take this personally, but this is my problem. I want to handle it on my own."

"Is it Beatrice Hamilton?" Mia ventured. "Is she still threatening to break up you and Toby?"

Carleen walked over to her desk, her back to Mia.

"She's determined to stop our marriage. I just have to hang on a little while longer. Then no one will be able to interfere in my life again."

Mia heard the strain in her voice and regretted pushing her for an answer, knowing how much pressure Carleen was under. "If there's anything I can do to help, please don't hesitate to ask me. Okay?"

Carleen turned around with a tremulous smile on her lips. "Okay."

"Now let's talk about something more pleasant."

"Like Nate?" Carleen ventured.

Mia wasn't ready to confide to her friend about her physical relationship with Nate—at least not until she understood it herself. "Actually, I meant our new client."

"Really?" Carleen exclaimed. "Hey, that's great news. The advertising must be paying off already. What's the job?"

"He wants to turn his basement into a game room."

Carleen plucked a piece of wrapped candy from the bowl on the desk. "Sounds like fun."

Mia shrugged. "I have a feeling he's going to be a high-maintenance client, but I can handle him. Though I'm not sure how to handle his collection of beer cans."

The candy slipped out of her hand and onto the floor. "What?"

"He collects beers from around the world and he wants to showcase the empty cans in his new game room."

"That's weird." Carleen bent down to pick the candy up. "So when do you start?"

"I told him I'd have some plans drawn up by the end of the week. But I'm not even going to start until he hands over the retainer. He's supposed to drop it off sometime this afternoon."

"Are you sure you want the job?" Carleen rounded the desk and sat down in her chair. "He sounds like he might be difficult."

"I'm hardly in a position to refuse. Besides, I can handle Mr. Kowalski."

"So that's his name?"

Mia nodded. "Sam Kowalski—beer can collector extraordinaire."

Carleen booted up the computer. "Interesting hobby. How common is it, do you suppose?"

"I dated a guy in college once who kept every beer bottle he ever drank," Mia replied. "He even built a ledge around the room to place them on. That's what got me interested in interior design."

Carleen looked up at her with amusement. "His beer bottle collection inspired you?"

"No, it horrified me. I knew then it was my mission to fix rooms like that one." Mia sighed. "Now it seems I've come full circle, thanks to Mr. Kowalski."

"He might not be back," Carleen ventured. "The retainer scares some of them away."

"Well, despite his taste in decor, I'm not in the position to be picky about my clients." Mia plopped down on the sofa. "So have you heard from Toby lately?"

Carleen's face brightened at her fiancé's name, melting all the tension lines away. "He called me last night around midnight. Oh, Mia, I miss him so much!"

"Is he coming home soon?"

"In just over a week. I know that's not that long, but it seems like forever to me. They've finished shooting most of the scenes, but have some cleanup work to do. Whatever that means."

"It means you're that much closer to becoming Mrs. Tobias Hamilton."

Carleen breathed a wistful sigh. "I hope so."

"You still haven't told me where you two are going for your honeymoon."

"It's a secret," Carleen said. "We don't want anyone to know where to find us."

"I guess I don't blame you for wanting a little privacy," Mia said, her thoughts drifting to Nate once again. "Especially from Toby's mother."

"If she had her way, she'd probably come with us," Carleen said with a sigh. Then shook her head. "No, if she had her way, I wouldn't even be in the picture."

"Let's forget about her," Mia said, determined to do something to help the situation, even if just by distracting her friend from it. "Why don't we go out for lunch? We'll put it on the company expense account."

"Since when do we have an expense account?"

"It's called positive thinking," Mia said, taking a bill out of her hands. "If we act like we have an expense account, then maybe we'll make enough money to start one."

She shook her head. "I can't argue with that logic."

An hour later, they returned to the house. But when Carleen pulled her car into the driveway, she left the motor running. "Hey, if you don't mind, I'd like to go run a few wedding errands."

"No, I don't mind," Mia replied, a little surprised that Carleen hadn't mentioned anything about it during lunch. "Would you like some company?"

She hesitated. "Thanks, but I'll probably get more accomplished if I'm on my own. I can stop by the fabric store and pick up those drapery swatches for the Keene job on my way."

"All right," Mia agreed, opening the car door. "I'm sure I can handle the office until you get back."

"I'll hurry," Carleen promised.

Mia climbed out of the car, then closed the door and watched Carleen back out of the driveway and peel away.

"What's going on with you?" Mia muttered to herself. She watched the car disappear before turning around and walking toward the door.

That's when she saw another car on the street. A familiar vintage Mustang. Heading her way. When she saw the man behind the wheel, her breath caught in her throat.

Nate Cafferty was making good on his promise.

12

NATE SAW CARLEEN walk into the house, though he was almost sure that she'd seen him driving down the street. He pulled into the driveway and cut the engine. Maybe he'd misread her last night. No. Not possible. He'd had enough experience with women to know she wasn't faking it. He'd brought her to climax and she'd enjoyed it.

So had he. That was the problem. He was mixing business with pleasure—big time. When he'd woken up this morning to find the bed empty beside him, he'd taken it personally, not giving a damn about the case.

But try as he might, he still couldn't figure out why she'd run out on him this morning without a word. Guilt for cheating on her rich fiancé, perhaps? Or for betraying Ian?

There was only one way to find out.

Nate walked up to the front door and rang the bell. After a moment passed, he wondered if she was going to answer. Then the door swung open and she stood on the other side.

The deep blush on her cheeks told him she remembered everything they'd done together in the foyer where she now stood.

"Can I come in?"

"Of course."

He walked inside the house, glad to see that her boss wasn't around. Then he turned to face her. "What happened this morning?"

"Happened?" she echoed, brushing past him and walking into the living room.

"When I woke up, you were gone."

She bent over the sofa to straighten a pillow. "I had a busy day planned."

"Carleen, look at me."

She slowly stood upright and turned to face him.

"If you want to forget what happened between us yesterday, I won't hold it against you."

"It's not that," she began.

"Then what is it?"

She began to pace across the floor, obviously distraught about something. Nate yearned to take her in his arms and comfort her.

What was it about this woman that drew him? It didn't make sense. He knew she was engaged to another man. Knew that she'd been seeing Ian as well. Nate hated cheaters, yet he couldn't bring himself to hate her.

She took a deep breath. "I can't tell you. Not yet."

Frustration simmered inside of him—both sexual and professional. "Tell me what?"

She shook her head. "It's complicated, Nate. So complicated that *I'm* confused by everything that's happening here—that's happening between us."

He moved closer to her. "I won't hurt you, Carleen. You can trust me."

"I do trust you." She looked up into his eyes and he could see the raw struggle of emotions on her beautiful face. "Just please give me some time."

Nate placed his hands on her shoulders and then pulled her close. Her head fit neatly under his chin. "I'll give you anything you want, Carleen."

She sighed when he said her name, almost as if it bothered her to hear it.

The doorbell interrupted the moment and they pulled apart. Nate sucked in a deep breath while she answered the door, keenly disappointed that now was not the time to finish what they'd started last night.

Just the memory of her coming apart in his arms made his body harden. He fought for control, barely aware of her speaking to a man at the door. Nate wanted to make love to her again, but when she was ready. His own needs would just have to wait—even if it killed him.

She closed the door and walked back into the living room, a check in her hand. "That was a new client," she explained, placing the check on the desk. "He wants me to design a game room for him."

Nate smiled. "Really? Is Mia making you her apprentice?"

She hesitated. "A common mistake. Clients are always mistaking me for Mia."

He could tell she was rattled, but he didn't understand why. "Where is Mia today? I was hoping to talk to her about my bedroom."

"That's a good question," she replied. "To tell you the truth, Nate, I'm worried about her."

"What's the problem?"

"You remember how she disappeared from the furniture store yesterday?"

He nodded. "That seemed a little strange, but she had a good explanation."

"She had a good explanation this morning, too, when I came home to find her gone. No note. No one here to answer the telephone. She's the most dependable person I know, yet she hasn't been acting like it lately."

"Have you asked her if something's bothering her?"

She gave a small shrug. "She blames it on stress. Business hasn't been good."

"Do you want me to talk to her?"

She blinked up at him in surprise. "You would do that?"

"Sometimes it's easier to talk to a stranger than a friend. Maybe she just doesn't want to worry you."

"That would be like her," she replied, then shook her head. "But I'm not sure it's such a good idea. As I said before, it's...complicated."

Nate had no choice but to follow her wishes, though he wondered if Mia's behavior had anything to do with Carleen. Maybe Mia's own suspicions had been raised about her office assistant and the black hole that was her past. Could Mia be conducting an investigation of her own?

That thought bothered him, bringing out his protective instincts. He didn't want anyone else snooping around Carleen's life—even her friends. If there was something she was hiding, *he* wanted to be in a position to help her. Which meant he had to discover her secrets before anyone else did.

"I'm here if you want me, Carleen," he said softly. "Just say the word."

They both knew he wasn't talking about her friend anymore. Nate almost regretted the words when he saw the flicker of indecision in her brown eyes again. He wanted to be the solution, not the problem.

Despite the temptation, he left without kissing her. He couldn't trust himself not to turn it into something more. And he knew she wasn't ready yet. He might need to go swimming in the Delaware River to cool off, but he'd wait until the right moment to make his move.

The moment she finally trusted him with the truth.

MIA LASTED ten long days and ten torturous nights before she knew it was time to end the masquerade. She simply couldn't hold out anymore. Not when she found herself sleeping beside Nate every night—desperate to feel his touch on her body again. Desperate to confide in him.

He'd backed off, pushing her neither physically nor emotionally, sensing something was bothering her. Part of her feared that he'd back off completely if she wasn't honest with him soon.

But coming clean about her masquerade presented another problem, this one to her business. Mia's Makeovers couldn't afford to reimburse Dr. Longo yet. Even with the new clients the advertising was bringing her, she'd used most of that money to pay her debts. But how could she ask him to keep that kind of secret from his foster father?

"Earth to Mia."

She looked up from the design plans in her lap to see Carleen staring at her. "Yes?"

"I said hello to you three times and you didn't answer me. Is something wrong?"

She shook her head. "It's nothing. You've got enough to deal with right now."

Carleen sat down beside her. "You don't have to tell me, I already know. It's Nate Cafferty, isn't it."

"Is it that obvious?"

"Only when you get that goofy look on your face and start to drool." Her smile widened. "Which seems to happen about twenty to thirty times a day."

Mia rolled her eyes. "I think you're exaggerating."

"And I think you're wild about the guy. So what's the problem?"

Mia set the design plans beside her on the sofa, grateful for a chance to finally confide in someone. "The problem is that he thinks I'm you. Do you know what it's like to have a man kiss you and make love to you, all the while calling you by another woman's name? I feel like such a phony."

A shadow crossed Carleen's face. "I think I know what you mean."

"I don't want to take our relationship any further until he knows the truth. But how can I tell him? Dr. Longo was his foster father and I'm sure he feels some loyalty to him. I don't want to put Nate in the position of having to choose between us."

Carleen sighed. "This is all my fault."

"No, it isn't," Mia countered. "I volunteered to take your place in the sleep study. Besides, if you had gone through with it, you'd be the one sleeping with Nate every night and I'd still be mooning over Ian."

"Speaking of Ian," Carleen said, "I'm surprised he hasn't been around here for a while."

"Me, too. Maybe I finally got through to him."

Carleen shook her head. "I doubt it, not with that ego of his. He's probably just biding his time, waiting to pounce again."

"I can't think about Ian right now," Mia replied. "I need to figure out what to do about Nate. I've already slipped up so many times. Pretty soon he's going to figure out the truth all on his own."

"Then you need to tell him and not worry about the consequences. If he tells Dr. Longo, so be it. Maybe the man won't care that you're Mia Maldonado instead of Carleen Wimmer. Why think the worst?"

"But what will Nate think? I've been lying to him since the day we met."

"But not maliciously," Carleen reminded her. "Why don't you just tell him the truth and find out what he thinks?"

Mia sucked in a deep breath. "All right. I will."

"THIS HAS GONE ON long enough, Nate. You need to tell her the truth."

Nate looked up at Harlan, who was watering the plants in his greenhouse laboratory. His foster father always had several scientific experiments going at once. Nate knew it was simply a way to keep busy and distract him from missing Adele.

Nate missed her, too. She was one of the few

women who had loved him unconditionally. Adele. His grandmother. Both gone forever. Just like Carleen would be if he didn't find a way to close this breach between them.

"She doesn't truly trust me yet," Nate replied. Though she'd told him she did, she hadn't been able to confide in him. "If she finds out I've been lying to her, she'll never trust me. I can't take that chance."

Harlan set down his watering can, his face grim. "Damn it, Nate, you're making a mistake here. And I don't like being a party to it."

"Does that mean you're going to tell her?"

Harlan hesitated, then shook his head. "It's not my place to interfere. You're an adult now. I just hate seeing you make the same mistakes you did when you were a teenager. Mistakes that could break your heart."

"Most women say I don't have a heart."

Harlan scowled. "That's not true and we both know it. You just keep it under lock and key so it won't get stomped to bits. That's no way to live, Nate. No way to love."

"It's my way."

"I know how much your mother hurt you, but this isn't the answer."

His gut tightened. "I don't want to talk about my mother."

"You never do," Harlan said softly. "Yet she's always here, guiding everything you do. She failed you, Nate. There's no excuse for what she did. But it's time you stopped punishing yourself for it."

"I'm just doing my job."

"Then you won't care if Carleen hates you when she finds out you've just been using her."

His smile faded. "I'm not using her."

"Aren't you? You're pumping her for information, no doubt using every means possible." Harlan picked up his watering can once again. "And for what? To break up two people in love. That's not right."

"I have very good reason to believe Carleen doesn't love her fiancé."

Harlan slowly rained water from the can onto his favorite hybrid peace lily, the one he'd named after his wife. "So you're telling me she *is* a gold digger?"

"No," he said hastily. "She's…confused."

"No doubt you're adding to that confusion. I've seen the way that woman looks at you, Nate. She's not confused, she's in love with you. You've done your job well."

Harlan always had a way of making Nate face a truth he didn't want to see. He'd done it when Nate was a teenager, too. Not forcing him into a corner, but making him look at a situation from every angle to keep him from rushing headlong into disaster.

Only this time Harlan was wrong.

Nate truly believed that breaking up Carleen's engagement was a good thing. She didn't need a witch like Beatrice Hamilton in her life. And her fiancé obviously didn't care enough about her to stop the damage his mother could do. The man had fled the country.

"I won't hurt her, Harlan," Nate vowed. "I care about her too much."

Harlan met his gaze. "I know you do, Nate. That's what worries me the most."

Nate didn't stick around to hear more. He had a plan and he'd come too far to let Harlan or his own doubts stop him now. He could sense a change in Carleen. A feeling that she was about to confide in him. To finally trust him.

But time was running out. The sleep study would be over in only six days and Tobias Hamilton would be back in Philadelphia. He couldn't afford to wait much longer.

MIA LAY in the predawn shadows of the Elvis suite, trying to work up the courage to tell Nate the truth. He'd been so sweet tonight when she'd come to bed, sensing the tension in her and offering her a back massage.

She'd been expecting more, almost disappointed when his hands hadn't strayed from her back and neck. But his tender touch had relaxed her so much, melting her anxieties away, that she'd fallen asleep before she could work up the courage to tell him the truth.

Now, with morning almost upon them, she questioned her timing. The sleep study would be over in just a few more days. Why not wait? At least then, if he was disgusted by her deception, she wouldn't have to face him every night.

The jukebox softly played "Can't Help Falling in Love" as she pondered her options. But there was no way to make her deception sound noble. She'd lied to him and she'd lied to Harlan Longo. If Nate never wanted to see her again, she wouldn't be able to blame him.

The mattress creaked and Nate's body rolled against her back. His chest pressed against her spine and shoulder blades, his hips cradling her buttocks. He circled one strong arm around her waist, drawing her even closer against him.

"Carleen, I lied to you."

His words, the same words she'd been rehearsing to say to him, startled her. "What do you mean?"

"I told you I was willing to wait. But the truth is, I can't wait. I've wanted you every second since that night. I want you so much that I can't stand it anymore."

She could feel the evidence of his words in the hard heat of his arousal. "I feel the same way."

"Then what are we waiting for?" he whispered, dropping butterfly kisses along the nape of her neck. "Come home with me."

She swallowed hard, seriously tempted. "We need to talk first."

"We'll talk at my house," he promised. "Where no one can interrupt us. Just say you'll come with me."

"I'll come with you," she echoed, telling herself it would be easier to confide in him outside of the sleep lab.

But they didn't make it to Nate's house. They barely made it out the door of the sleep lab before they were in each other's arms, frantic to make up for the precious days they'd lost.

They only made it halfway across the estate when Nate scooped her up in his arms and carried her to the abandoned school bus. He kicked a chicken out of his path, then climbed aboard, his gaze roaming over the dilapidated interior before he settled on a spot at the very back of the bus—a long padded bench that stretched across the width of the bus.

"The security cameras..." she said with a trace of unease.

"They can't see anything in here," he assured her. "No one will know." His voice trailed off and his face contorted in anguish. "We'll go to my house," he said, his breath coming in uneven rasps. "We'll find a better place...."

"No." She pulled his head down for a long, wet kiss. Then she said, "I don't want to wait a second more."

It was the truth. After denying herself for so many nights, she just wanted to lose herself in his heat again. The moment he laid her on the seat, they were in each other's arms, lips meeting, hands moving. Urgent moans filled the empty bus as they surrendered to the passion that still burned so hotly between them.

Nate's promise to himself to go slowly evaporated the moment she reached for the fly of his jeans. Desire made him swell to almost painful proportions, a condition that only her touch could alleviate.

A smile played on her lips as she slowly slid the zipper all the way down, then caressed the length of him through his boxer shorts. Once. Twice. Three times. He closed his eyes and moaned aloud, so on fire for her that he couldn't think straight.

But he could still feel and touch and taste. He leaned forward, pulling her top and bra over her head in one fluid movement. Then he feasted on her breasts, first lavishing his favor on one nipple until it peaked in his mouth, then turning his attention to the other.

She twined her hands in his hair, pulling him closer as her entire body trembled with need. The awkwardness of the space seemed insignificant compared to the sexual heat blazing between them.

Moisture condensed on the windows as their kisses turned lush and long. He stroked his hands over her breasts and then lower, over her smooth belly.

Nate knew he couldn't hold out much longer. He reached into the pocket of his jeans and pulled out a condom, his fingers shaking slightly as he fumbled with the foil wrapper.

When he turned back to her, she was ready for him, wearing only her pink bikini panties. The sight of her like that melted any last reservations he might have about making love to her in this old bus.

He pulled her on top of him, the crux of her thighs meeting his erection. The sensation of those silk panties against his sensitive flesh almost proved too much for him. He arched against her, slipping his hands inside her panties and squeezing her perfect bottom.

Then he pulled off the panties and heard a soft sigh of longing waft from her lips. He kissed her, exploring her sweet mouth as his fingers dipped inside of her.

She moaned her pleasure into his mouth, so he did it again, the pressure mounting inside of him. Her body began to tremble on top of him, her hips rocking against his groin in the most erotic way he'd ever experienced.

He let the moment linger, both of them teetering on the edge. "I need you," he breathed, seeing the raw desire in her brown eyes. Feeling her warm, uneven breathing against his cheek.

Then he kissed her, trying to tell her without words just how much he needed her. Not just now, but forever.

She sank down on top of him, slowly filling her body with his hard length. He moaned aloud at the acuteness of the sensation, his head lolling back against the seat.

Then she began to move on him, faster and faster, until Nate lost all control. He drove into her, matching her rhythm. She gripped his shoulders, her fingers pressing into his skin as tiny whimpers emanated from her throat. The sound inflamed him, and he struggled not to surrender to the sweet ecstasy until she came with him.

"Now, love," he urged, his fingers slipping between the cleft of her buttocks until he found the place their bodies joined together as one. He kneaded and stroked the tender skin, encouraged by the cries rising in her throat.

Drops of condensation trickled down the windows, but nothing could distract him from the woman on top of him. She clenched him once, twice, then fell against his chest as the waves of pleasure overtook her. He followed a moment later, shouting out the name now branded on his heart.

Carleen.

13

NATE WASN'T SURE how much time had passed before he was able to move again. Carleen lay atop him, both of them damp with sweat. He felt like a teenager again. Here he was, almost thirty, and he hadn't even been able to wait until they found a bed.

Carleen did that to him. That and more. More than he wanted to admit.

"Wow," she said at last. "I didn't know it was supposed to be like that."

He smiled into her hair. "I'll take that as a compliment."

She splayed one hand over his bare chest. "You're an incredible man, Nate Cafferty."

A small pang of guilt shot through him. She wouldn't say that if she knew the truth. He'd seduced her. Carrying out a cold, calculated plan to wreck her engagement. Now he had to find a way to minimize the damage without losing her in the process.

"But I do have a confession to make," she said, her voice growing solemn. "One you may not want to hear."

"Hey," he said, placing one finger on her chin and tipping it up so her gaze met his. "You don't ever have to be afraid of me. I think I'm falling in love with you, Carleen."

Tears filled her eyes. "You might be falling in love with me. Oh, Nate, I hope you are. But you're not falling for Carleen Wimmer."

Tension knotted his gut. So she was about to admit the truth. He'd known Carleen was an alias. He just hoped he was prepared to hear all the rest. "Tell me."

"I will," she promised. "But I want you to take me home first. There's something there that you have to see."

Nate chafed at the delay, but he owed her at least that much. They pulled their clothes back on, an uncomfortable tension now settling between them.

Nate hated it. Almost as much as he hated the thought of telling Carleen the real reason he'd been her bed partner in the sleep study.

How could he tell her he was being paid to ruin her?

MIA KNEW she was just putting off the inevitable, but if Nate decided to shut her out of his life when she told him the truth, she'd rather be in her own home. Her gut tightened as she unlocked the front door and walked inside, not ready to face that possibility.

Nate followed her, closing the door behind him. Then he took her in his arms. "Tell me what's going on, Carleen. Don't be afraid. I have a few secrets of my own."

She sucked in a deep breath. "I'm not Carleen."

Mia waited for him to recoil in shock, but Nate didn't seem all that surprised. He pulled her closer, kissing the top of her head.

Still holding her, he pulled away just far enough to look into her eyes. "Then who are you?"

"I'm Mia."

His arms stiffened around her. "What?"

She stepped away from him, realizing nothing she could have done would have prepared her for his reaction. Not the shock on his handsome face. Not the betrayal in his green eyes. "My name is Mia Maldonado."

He stared at her for several long moments. "What kind of game is this?"

"The real Carleen and I switched identities for the sleep study."

Nate turned away from her, rubbing one hand over his jaw. "I don't believe this."

"I'm sorry," she said, staring at the broad expanse of his back. "I know I lied to you, but I truly didn't mean any harm. I just wanted to take Carleen's place in the sleep study and I figured the easiest way to do it was to pretend that I was her."

He slowly turned around, his expression implacable. "So let me get this straight. Mia is really Carleen and you're really Mia?"

She nodded, feeling slightly sick inside. "Yes."

"Since when?"

"Since the sleep study started," she replied, "just over two weeks ago."

He stared at her, as if unable to make the connection. "You're Mia Maldonado? You've *always been* Mia Maldonado?"

She'd expected him to be surprised, even angry, but the depth of his shock perplexed her. "Since the day I was born."

"Why did you wait this long to tell me?"

She took a deep breath. "Because I was afraid you'd tell Dr. Longo and he'd ask for his stipend back. Mia…I mean, Carleen, had already spent it on advertising on my business. I just can't afford to pay him back right now."

Nate stood there, letting her words sink in. "So you're not the office assistant here—you're the owner."

"That's right." She couldn't believe this was the same man who had made such sweet love to her less than an hour ago. He made no move to hold her or kiss her. Uttered no words of reassurance that her lie didn't matter.

"Tell me why."

She gave a slight shrug. "It doesn't really matter…."

"It matters to me," he insisted.

She walked into the living room, trying to compose herself. What did she expect after deceiving him night after night? Nate didn't strike her as a man who tolerated someone making a fool of him and that's exactly what she had done.

Mia turned around to face him, ready to accept the consequences of her actions. Even if it meant losing him. "Carleen is engaged to a very wealthy man named Toby Hamilton. They're getting married soon and she won't be working for me after their wedding. But she felt bad about leaving the business when we're barely making ends meet."

"So she used the sleep study money to buy advertising for Mia's Makeovers," Nate deduced.

She nodded. "I had no idea that was her plan until

she told me the day the sleep study was to begin. Toby was upset that she was going to participate." Mia started pacing across the floor, wanting him to understand. "Carleen's been so stressed lately, I thought I could help by volunteering to go in her place."

"But why pretend you're Carleen? Why not just go as yourself?"

"We had no reason to believe Harlan would accept me. Especially after he had Carleen fill out that detailed personality profile that asked all those personal questions. The contract made it clear that if Carleen didn't show up, she'd have to give back all the money. The money we didn't have anymore."

"Then why didn't she ask her fiancé for the money? You said he was rich."

"I know, but that's a very sore subject for her. Toby's mother is convinced she's a gold digger, so Carleen has made it a point never to ask him for a dime."

Nate whistled low. "I can't believe I never suspected a thing."

She took a deep breath. "Can you ever forgive me?"

Nate looked at her for so long that Mia's heart sank. She'd finally met Mr. Right and then blown it. Finally found the love of her life and lost him, with no one to blame but herself.

"Forgive you?" he echoed, his voice tight. "No."

She gave a sharp nod. "I understand."

"No, I don't think you do." He reached for her hands. "I don't forgive you, because there's nothing to forgive. I'm just so damn glad the woman I love isn't engaged to another man."

Hope sparked inside of her. "Really?"

"I'll admit the fact that you're not Carleen is a bit of a shock," he said, pulling her closer. "But I should have figured that out for myself."

"Neither Carleen nor I are very good actresses, are we?"

"You made a few slipups," he agreed, "now that I think about it. But I was too distracted to notice."

"Distracted?"

He drew her into his arms. "Distracted by you... my beautiful Mia."

She smiled. "I love hearing you say my name."

"Mia," he repeated again. "My Mia."

Then he kissed her.

Joy swelled inside of her as she wrapped her arms around his neck. The burden she'd been carrying for the last two weeks had finally been lifted.

"Let me go upstairs and tell Carleen," Mia said, ready to share her good news with the world. "I'm sure she'll be relieved that you finally know the truth."

He nodded. "I'll wait right here for you."

She kissed him again, then bounded up the stairs. But her joy quickly faded when she reached Carleen's room. The door was flung open and chaos lay inside.

Half the dresser drawers were on the floor, all of them empty. The bed was unmade, the mattress hung askew at a crazy angle. Shards of shattered glass lay glistening in the sunlight on the hardwood floor.

Mia walked over to carefully picked up the photo,

turning it over to see a picture of Tobias Hamilton smiling confidently at her.

The strong odor of her roommate's favorite perfume assailed her nostrils. Mia saw the bottle lying on its side on the dresser, the aromatic liquid pooled underneath.

Either Carleen had packed up and left in a hurry— or someone had taken her.

NATE STOOD ALONE in the living room wondering if he should give up his private investigator's license. Those two women had completely fooled him. He'd been investigating Mia Maldonado all these weeks, not Carleen Wimmer.

But his chagrin was overshadowed by a sense of exaltation. The woman he'd fallen in love with hadn't been cheating on her fiancé. She didn't even *have* a fiancé.

But what did he do now? He was no closer to solving the mystery of Carleen Wimmer than when he'd begun.

Mia appeared at the top of the stairs, her face ghostly pale. "Carleen's gone."

"What do you mean?"

"Something happened. Her room is a mess and some of her clothes are missing. Either she left in a panic or someone took her against her will."

Nate ran up the stairs two at a time to join her, then took her hand. She led him to Carleen's room and he knew as soon as he saw it that she hadn't been exaggerating.

Something was *very* wrong.

"Has anything like this ever happened before?" he asked, taking a quick inventory of the room. It was in complete disarray, but he didn't see any blood or any other signs that she'd been hurt.

"No, never."

"Does she have a suitcase?"

Mia walked toward the closet. "She usually keeps it on the upper shelf, but I don't see it here now."

"Good. That's a good sign that she left of her own free will."

Mia turned to face. "But why would she leave without telling me? Why would her room look like this? Carleen's one of the tidiest people I know."

Nate didn't say anything, wondering if now was the time to come clean about his own deception. But Mia was already distraught. She might even think he had something to do with Carleen's sudden disappearance if he confessed his connection to Beatrice Hamilton.

Then another thought occurred to him. What if Beatrice Hamilton was behind this? Had she gotten impatient waiting for Nate to complete his investigation and threatened Carleen in some way?

There was only one way to find out.

"Look," he began. "I have some friends in the police department. I'm going to put out some feelers and see what I can find out."

"I'll go with you."

That was the last thing he wanted. "No, I think you should stay here in case Carleen calls or tries to contact you."

"Why didn't she confide in me?" Mia cried. "I've

known for weeks that something's been bothering her. Now it might be too late."

He pulled her into his arms, wishing he could tell her everything was going to be all right. But he simply didn't have enough information yet. "I'll be back as fast as I can."

She nodded bravely, swallowing back her tears. "Thank you, Nate."

He kissed her, long and hard. When he left, she was sitting on Carleen's bed, staring at the disaster that had been left behind.

"I'll make it all up to you, Mia," he promised her under his breath, "if it's the last thing I do."

THE HAMILTON ESTATE was nestled in one of Philadelphia's most exclusive gated communities, but Nate didn't wait to be announced. He stormed past the butler, finding his client in the solarium.

Beatrice sat in front of an antique needlepoint stand with a vertical frame. A large pastel tapestry was stretched taut between the wooden scroll bars. She presented the picture of a genteel lady from centuries past, sweet and stately.

But Nate knew there was no way "sweet" described Beatrice Hamilton.

Her patrician brow arched when she saw Nate. "This is a surprise, Mr. Cafferty. A pleasant one, I hope. Do you have some good news for me?"

"Carleen Wimmer is missing."

She smiled. "That is very good news indeed."

"I want to know if you're behind her disappearance."

She secured her needle in the fabric, then rose from her chair. "I don't allow my employees to use that kind of tone with me."

"Then you'll be happy to know that I no longer work for you."

She nodded. "I accept your resignation, since it appears your mission has been accomplished. Tell me, how did you drive the little harlot away?"

Nate clenched his jaw. He'd come here hoping that Beatrice Hamilton could shed some light on Carleen's sudden disappearance. He'd even convinced himself that she'd been behind it. But either she was an excellent actress or she didn't know anything.

"I was hoping you could tell me," Nate said.

She lifted her shoulders in a regal shrug. "Getting rid of that pest was your job, Mr. Cafferty. One, if I may remind you, that I paid you quite handsomely for."

"You can have your money back," he replied. "I never should have taken this job."

She nodded. "Ms. Wimmer has gotten to you, I see. Just as she did with my son. It seems she has quite a talent for making men fall in love with her."

Nate knew he was wasting his time here, but he wanted to ask one more question before he left.

"Why do you hate Carleen so much?"

She didn't even hesitate. "Because she isn't worthy of my son or the Hamilton name. She is a nobody. Certainly not a fitting mother for my future grandchildren."

Nate had been born to a mother who didn't care anything about him, choosing to bestow all her affection on a bottle of booze. Now he saw the damage of the other extreme. Beatrice Hamilton's love for her son bordered on suffocation. Yet both his mother and Tobias Hamilton's mother shared something in common—neither was capable of unconditional love.

"Now if you'll excuse me, Mr. Cafferty, I must get back to my needlework."

He turned and walked out of the room without another word. He owed an apology to Tobias Hamilton.

And he owed the truth to Mia Maldonado.

14

FOR THE NEXT three hours, Mia's heart jumped every time the phone rang. Normally, she'd be thrilled to have so many potential clients call to ask her for more information about her business. But today she just wanted to hear from Carleen.

Time dragged by with no word from Carleen or Nate. She busied herself with cleaning, something she usually avoided. But worry gnawed at her. By the time she'd finished dusting and polishing and scrubbing, the house sparkled.

As she cleaned, Mia tried to come up with every possible scenario that could explain Carleen's mysterious disappearance. She even tried to reach Toby on an overseas call to Frankfurt. When he didn't answer, she hung up the phone, half frustrated, half relieved.

Toby might have been able to tell her where Carleen had gone, since they phoned or e-mailed each other practically every night. On the other hand, he might have flown home in a panic, only to discover that Mia overreacted.

She took a deep breath and surveyed her newly sanitized living room. Maybe she *was* overreacting. Her own emotions had been in turmoil lately. Sleeping with Nate every night had definitely taken a toll on her equilibrium. Plus, she'd been trying to save her business and lose her ex-boyfriend.

Maybe Carleen had been sending out signals Mia hadn't seen. Or perhaps Beatrice Hamilton's endless harassment had finally driven Carleen away.

The doorbell rang and her heart leapt into her throat. She ran to the door, but found the last person she wanted to see standing on the other side.

"Hello, Ian."

"I need to talk to you," he said, brushing by her without waiting for an invitation to come inside.

She was in no mood to deal with him. "This really isn't a good time."

"There is no good time for what I have to say. It's about your new boyfriend."

"Nate?"

"That's right." He held up a file folder. "Nate Cafferty is not what he appears to be."

"Ian—" she began.

"Just hear me out," he interjected. "If after I'm done, you want me to leave, then I'll leave."

She recognized the stubborn gleam in his eye and knew she'd get rid of him faster if she just let him have his way.

"Fine," she said, waving him inside. "But please make it quick."

Ian slapped the folder in his hand. "I took the liberty of conducting a little research on your friend Nate."

"He's more than a friend," she replied, wanting to make that perfectly clear. "And what do you mean by research?"

"I hired a private investigator to check him out."

She blanched. "You what?"

"It wasn't easy," he said, oblivious to her indignation. "There must be some kind of unwritten code among private investigators not to spy on each other. But I finally found one who wasn't burdened by such scruples."

She shook her head. "Well, there's your first mistake. Nate isn't a private investigator, he's a security specialist."

Ian snorted. "Is that what he told you?"

"That's the truth."

He smiled affectionately at her. "You've always been so trusting—so innocent. That's one of the reasons I fell in love with you."

She thought about how she'd made love with Nate on the old school bus—she'd been far from innocent then. Which just proved that Ian didn't know her at all.

"And probably the reason you felt you could cheat on me." Mia wished the words back as soon as she'd spoken them. Their past relationship simply didn't matter to her anymore. "Actually, Ian, I believe it all worked out for the best. For me, anyway."

Frustration knit his brow. "I know I hurt you, Mia, and I'm sorry. That's one of the reasons I'm not going to let this Cafferty hurt you, too."

"Nate won't hurt me."

"How can you be so sure? After all, he does have a police record."

Mia looked at him in disbelief as he pulled a sheaf of paper from the file folder.

"It's all right here," he said, handing it to her.

She quickly skimmed the report. "This happened years ago. Back when he was a teenager."

"He was convicted for property damage, assault and resisting arrest. He spent a considerable amount of time in juvenile hall."

She shoved the paper back at him. "Ancient history."

"The guy's a loser, Mia. Hell, even his own mother tossed him out of her life."

Her heart clenched. "What do you mean?"

"His mother disowned him—legally. Turned him over to the state. After he got out of juvenile hall, he was put into the foster care system."

She thought about Nate's house, devoid of family photographs. He didn't have any because he didn't have a family. Not one that wanted him, anyway.

"I know this is hard to hear," Ian said, gentling his tone. "But I wanted you to find out before you got in too deep with this guy."

She met his gaze. "It's too late."

Ian moved toward her. "No. That can't be true. He caught you on the rebound. You don't even really know the man."

"I know everything I need to know," she retorted. "Nate is a decent, honest man. A man I can trust."

Ian reached out and grasped her shoulders. "Listen to yourself, Mia! You only met this guy a few weeks ago. You don't know him at all."

"Please just give it up, Ian. We're through."

He pulled her to him. "I'm the one who loves you. I'm the one you need."

She squirmed in his grasp, more angry than afraid. Why had she ever wasted a moment of her time wishing this man back into her life? "I think you should go."

"Let's start over," he proposed. "We can pretend none of this ever happened. I believe we could make it work."

"It's too late," she repeated, almost feeling sorry for him. His inability to let go of what he wanted almost seemed like a sickness. "I don't want to see you again. I don't want you spying on me or on Nate. If you do, I'll tell him about it. And I don't think he's a man you want to cross."

Ian stared at her for a long moment, as if trying to decide whether to take her threat seriously. At last, he said, "You'll want me back. Nate's true colors will show sooner or later. A man like that doesn't change. When you realize your mistake, just give me a call."

She watched him try to hang on to some tiny shred of dignity as he turned around and walked out of her house. She knew in her gut that he'd never be back. A man like Ian Brock didn't take humiliation well.

Feeling physically drained, she closed the door, wishing Nate was here right now. Ian had left the file folder on the coffee table. She picked it up to toss it in the waste basket, but several photographs slipped out and fell on the floor.

She bent down to gather them up, her gaze falling on an image that looked familiar. It was a picture of her entering Cavalli's restaurant, wearing her favorite blue dress. Then she saw what looked like Nate's car parked along the curb opposite the restaurant.

The man hunched behind the wheel wore sunglasses and a ball cap, but she could almost swear it was him.

Taking a seat on the floor, she studied each photograph. There was one of Nate walking just outside the Longo estate. Another of him pruning his rosebushes. Each one seemed innocuous, but something about them made her uneasy. She just couldn't put her finger on it.

She looked at the last picture, which looked as if it had been taken through a wrought-iron fence. She could see Nate speaking with a middle-aged woman, his back half turned to the camera. Shaking her head, she tapped the photos together, then threw them in the trash with the file folder.

The fact that she'd let Ian make her question Nate, even for a moment, angered her. Nate's past didn't matter to her. He was a survivor. The fact that he'd been through so much only made her love him more.

The telephone rang and she picked it up. "Hello?"

"Mia, it's Nate."

She smiled her relief into the phone. "I'm so glad it's you."

"Listen, we need to talk."

"Have you found out something about Carleen?"

He hesitated. "We're due at the sleep lab in about an hour. Why don't we meet there? We can talk all night."

She'd completely forgotten about the sleep study. "I'm not sure I can stand waiting even that long. Have you heard anything about Carleen?"

"No," he replied. "But I did notify the police. They're going to check all the hospitals in the area and keep an eye out for her car."

"So what did you want to talk to me about?" she asked.

"Not over the phone," he told her. "This is something that needs to be said face-to-face."

Another wave of uneasiness washed over her. "Should I be concerned?"

His long hesitation didn't make her feel any better. "There's something important you need to know."

Then the line disconnected. Mia listened to the dial tone drone in her ear for several moments before she replaced the cordless phone on the base unit. Nate hadn't said he loved her. He hadn't even said goodbye.

A strange chill ran though her bones, but she shook it off. Ian's visit and the way he'd tried to smear Nate had unsettled her. She'd feel better when she saw him. When he held her in his arms.

Mia wouldn't let Ian or anyone else ever make her doubt him again.

AN HOUR AFTER his phone call to Mia, Nate entered the sleep lab.

"Good evening, Mr. Cafferty." Hannah stood in the center hub, a clipboard in one hand. "How are you?"

"I'm fine," he lied. "Has...Carleen arrived yet?" He'd caught himself just in time, almost slipping up by calling Mia by her real name. Not that it really mattered. Harlan wouldn't care about the deception. He'd probably be amused by it. But Nate wanted Mia to have the chance to tell Harlan herself.

Hannah shook her head. "Not yet. I'm expecting

her soon, though. She's one of the few punctual research subjects in the study."

Yes, his Mia was punctual. She was also smart, creative and sexy as hell. He just hoped she was forgiving. Because he intended to confess everything to her tonight.

Hannah set the clipboard on the counter. "Hey, you two disappeared this morning before I had a chance to talk to you."

"Sorry about that," Nate said, though he wasn't sorry at all. He'd never walk past that old bus again without remembering how Mia had ridden him on the backseat. His body tightened just thinking about it.

"It wasn't a problem for me," Hannah clarified, "but I wanted to tell Carleen about a phone call that came in for her last night."

Nate approached the hub. "A phone call?"

"It was well after midnight." Hannah looked down to check the phone log. "The biomonitor readings indicated that Carleen was already in a sound sleep. So I told the caller I didn't want to wake her, even if it was her boss."

His heart skipped a beat. "Her boss? You mean Mia Maldonado?"

Hannah nodded. "That's right. I was surprised she was calling here so late, but people keep all kinds of strange hours these days."

Adrenaline shot through him. It had to be the missing Carleen who had called. Because the real Mia Maldonado had been sleeping beside him last night.

"Did she leave any kind of message? Did she sound upset or scared? What did she say?"

Hannah's eyes widened at his rapid-fire questions. "I don't remember exactly. She identified herself, then asked to speak to Carleen. I told her that Carleen was already sleeping, but that I'd be happy to take a message."

"And?" Nate prodded.

"And she hung up." A buzzer sounded on the control panel, and Hannah fiddled with a button for a moment before it cut off. "That's why I wanted to mention it to Carleen this morning. I didn't want her to get in trouble with her boss."

Nate raked a hand through his hair. "I really wish you'd told us last night."

Hannah winced. "I'm sorry. Dr. Longo made it clear that he wanted as few outside interruptions as possible during the sleep study. If I'd known it was important—"

"It's not your fault," Nate interjected, wishing he hadn't taken his frustration out on her. "Look…it's complicated. But do me a favor. If a woman claiming to be Mia Maldonado does call again, please let us know right away. Okay?"

She nodded, looking more than a little confused by the request. "All right. Will do."

"Thanks, Hannah." He moved toward the Elvis suite, checking his watch. The real Mia was running late, which puzzled him since she'd seemed so impatient to talk to him when he'd phoned her earlier.

After another twenty minutes passed, his puzzlement turned to concern. He walked out of the Elvis suite and waited for Hannah to emerge from one of the other suites.

"Any word from Carleen?" he asked.

Hannah shook her head. "I tried calling her a few minutes ago, but the answering machine picked up. Maybe she's having car trouble or something."

It was the *or something* possibility that worried him.

"I'm going to look for her," he said, walking up to the hub and grabbing a notepad and pen off the counter. "Here's my cell phone number. If Carleen does show up, please give me a call right away."

"Good luck," Hannah called after him, shaking her head at his odd behavior.

Nate sincerely hoped he didn't need any luck. But the closer he got to Mia's house, the more worried he became. He'd taken the most direct route between her place and the Longo estate, but he hadn't spotted her car anywhere along the road. Which meant her delay wasn't caused by either a flat tire or an overheated engine.

When he finally reached her house, Nate was relieved to see her Miata in the driveway. But there was another car parked next to it. A red Lamborghini. Had a client delayed her? He knew she'd been desperately trying to drum up more business, but surely she would have called the sleep lab to let them know she'd be late.

Nate parked his car behind hers and then approached the house. The front door was closed, but he could hear a man shouting inside. The words were blurred, but they sounded both angry and desperate.

He barreled through the door, not bothering to knock. A lanky blond man stood in the center of the living room, his face flushed with rage. Mia stood behind the desk, her brown eyes wide with alarm.

"What the hell is going on here?" Nate demanded.

The man whirled on him. "That's what I want to know. Who are you?"

"None of your damn business." He placed himself between the man and Mia, then turned to her and asked, "Are you all right?"

"I'm fine," she said, reaching for his hand and giving it a reassuring squeeze. "But Toby is out of control."

"Toby?" Nate echoed, his gut tightening into a knot.

"Toby Hamilton," she clarified, nodding toward the man glaring at both of them. "Carleen's fiancé."

15

MIA WATCHED the color drain from Nate's face. "What's wrong?"

He shook his head. "Nothing."

She didn't believe him, but she had her hands full with Toby at the moment. He'd come bursting in here demanding to see Carleen over half an hour ago. When Mia told him that she'd packed her bags and left, he'd gone ballistic.

"Toby found out his mother hired some guy to romance Carleen away from him," Mia explained. "He's upset."

Toby snorted. "Upset? That's putting it mildly. I want to find that guy and rip his throat out. If I lose Carleen because of him…"

"Then you'll only have yourself to blame," Nate told him.

They both looked at him in surprise.

"What the hell is that supposed to mean?" Toby sputtered.

"It means," Nate replied, "that you left your fiancée here to fend for herself, didn't you? All the while knowing your mother had it in for her."

"Of course, I knew it," Toby retorted. "She hated

my fiancée. But Carleen is a strong woman. That's one of the things I love most about her."

Nate stared at him for a long moment. "Or maybe you just like to jerk your mother around, but don't have the courage to stick around when she jerks back."

Toby's jaw clenched as he turned to Mia. "Who is this guy?"

She struggled to find the right words to describe their relationship. "Nate and I have been seeing each other."

"Then this is none of your damn business," Toby said to Nate.

"I decided to make it my business when I heard you shouting at Mia." Nate stepped around the desk, his hands fisted at his sides. "You should be thanking her instead of berating her. She's done her best to help Carleen through this mess."

Toby visibly deflated. "I'm not mad at Mia. I just want to know what happened to Carleen. No one seems to be able to tell me anything except that she disappeared."

As Mia watched the two of them, something niggled at her brain. Some connection between Toby and Nate. But she couldn't seem to put it together.

Toby sank down on the sofa and buried his head in his hands. "What if it worked? What if she went off somewhere with this guy?"

Mia joined him there. "That's *not* what happened. Carleen loves you. She can't wait until your wedding day. I'll admit she'd been acting a little odd lately, but I really don't believe it had anything to do with another man."

Toby lifted his head to look at her. "Acting odd? What do you mean?"

Mia gave a slight shrug. "Moody. Unpredictable. Even a little paranoid. She'd disappear for short periods of time without telling anyone where she was going."

"That doesn't sound like my Carleen."

"That's why I found it odd," Mia replied. "I was worried about her, but she kept assuring me it was just a reaction from the stress of planning the wedding."

He closed his eyes. "I should have been here for her."

"So why weren't you?" Nate asked, not sounding the least bit sympathetic. "Maybe you could have stopped this situation before it spun out of control."

Toby shook his head. "You're wrong. Nothing would have stopped my mother from hiring that private investigator. But I took the coward's way out. I didn't want to take a stand against my mother."

His words hit Mia like a sudden onslaught of hail. "A private investigator?"

"Yeah," Toby affirmed. "She was quite proud of herself, certain she'd saved me from a life of misery. All thanks to the P.I. she hired to get Carleen out of my life."

Ian's photographs flashed in her mind. A photo of Nate parked outside the restaurant. Another photo of him standing inside a gated garden, speaking with a wealthy middle-aged woman. A woman who had to be about Beatrice Hamilton's age.

She thought about Nate's reaction when he'd discovered he'd been sleeping with Mia instead of Carleen. How he'd almost seemed more upset at himself than at her for not figuring it out sooner.

The pieces locked together in her mind with a sickening lurch.

She met Nate's gaze and the expression she saw on his face confirmed her worst fear. "You're him. You're the private investigator."

A muscle flicked in his jaw. "Yes."

Toby looked from one to the other.

"What are you talking about?"

But Mia barely heard him, all her attention on Nate. "Your participation in the sleep study was no accident, was it?" Numb from the shock, her voice sounded far away to her ears. "You were expecting to find Carleen Wimmer there. In fact, you and Harlan planned it that way. That's why she was invited to participate, wasn't it?"

Nate rounded the desk. "Mia, let me explain...."

But she wasn't about to give him a chance to talk his way out of this one. Not when she could figure it all out on her own. "And the fact that Carleen had a fiancée didn't stop you from pursuing her, did it? In fact, you were being paid to do just that."

He stopped in front of her, flinching at each word as if they were physical blows.

She rose to her feet. "All the time we were together, you were just trying to seduce me—the woman you thought was Carleen—away from Toby. And you probably thought you'd succeeded, until I told you my real identity."

"You're the guy?" Toby asked, finally catching on.

Nate nodded, his gaze fixed on Mia. "Beatrice

Hamilton hired me to dig up dirt on Carleen, but I'd hit a dead end. So when I heard about Harlan's new sleep study, I convinced him to send her an invitation. I thought if I got close to her, she'd trust me enough to tell me what I wanted to know."

He spoke without inflection, as if giving testimony in a trial. Only he was already guilty.

"And what did you want to know?" she asked, hating the quaver in her voice. The shock was fading, the void it left behind quickly filling with both rage and pain. She'd picked Mr. Wrong again. Only this time, he'd done more than break her heart. He'd crushed her soul.

Nate hesitated, glancing at Toby, then back at Mia again. "For one thing, I wanted to know why she'd been using an alias for the last year. Carleen Wimmer isn't her real name."

"Liar!" Toby exclaimed.

"It's true," Nate said evenly. "I did an extensive background check. Carleen Wimmer did not exist a year ago. At least, not the Carleen Wimmer we know."

"You don't know her," Mia bit out. "And how can we trust what you say? You've been deceiving both of us from the beginning. The job to redecorate your bedroom was just a ruse, just like everything else— an excuse to give you a reason to come into my home and snoop around."

"I was doing my job," Nate replied. "But I'm not proud of it."

Images flashed through her mind. Their first kiss. The first time they'd made love in this very foyer. The numerous times he'd made her come undone in his arms, like in that old school bus this morning.

All part of a calculated plan.

Mia should have trusted her first instincts about him—when she'd tagged him as a Mr. Wrong. He'd treated her no differently than Ian—who had also lied to her. Also deceived her while professing to care. *Hadn't she learned anything?*

Mia closed her eyes, nausea roiling inside of her. "I think I'm going to be sick."

Nate moved beside her. "Please don't do this to yourself. I never meant to hurt you. I was going to tell you everything tonight."

She opened her eyes and backed away from him. "Tonight? Sorry, Nate, but even if I buy that story, it's too little, too late."

Toby stood up to confront him. "So if you know so much about Carleen, tell me where I can find her now."

"That I don't know," he said bluntly.

Toby's eyes narrowed. "And I'm supposed to believe you? After all, my mother hired you. You're probably still on her payroll."

"I quit today," Nate replied.

"Yeah, after you found out Carleen had gone," Mia pointed out. "When your mission had been accomplished."

He rubbed one hand over his jaw. "It wasn't like that! If you'd just let me explain…."

"Go ahead," she challenged. "Tell me why I should ever believe *anything* you say to me. You've lied since the beginning."

"You lied too," he countered.

"Yes," she admitted. "I pretended to be Carleen Wimmer because I needed the money from the sleep study. Money to save my business. That was wrong. But at least I didn't lie to destroy other people's lives."

"I've got to find her," Toby muttered, starting to pace. "But I don't even know where to start looking!"

"She called the sleep lab last night," Nate announced, "looking for Mia."

Mia stared at him, feeling like a fool for trusting him. "You knew and didn't tell me? Even after you saw how frantic I was this morning?"

"I didn't know until I got to the sleep lab tonight," Nate clarified. "Hannah told me about the call. The point is that I set up the security system at the Longo estate—including the phone lines. We might be able to trace that call."

"So now you're offering to help." Mia just wanted him to leave so she could absorb everything that had happened. "After weeks of trying to break Carleen and Toby apart, you want to bring them back together again?"

"I want to make amends," Nate said.

"It's too late." Still shaky from the shock, Mia walked over to open the front door, hoping her legs would hold her long enough for him to leave. "Toby and I can handle it from here."

Nate started to argue, then gave up and walked to the door. He paused beside her, his green eyes beseeching. "Give me a second chance, Mia. I…love you."

She swallowed the sob in her throat, struggling to keep control. "Goodbye, Nate."

Tears blurred her vision and it took a moment before she realized he had gone. She stood by the open door, sucking in deep breaths of fresh air.

Toby joined her there. "Look, Mia, I know you're upset. I can see what that jerk did to you and I'm sorry. But I need you to do something for me."

She gave a shaky nod. "Anything."

"Stay here in case Carleen comes home or tries to call you again. I'm going to check every place we've ever been together in this city. Maybe someone saw her or can tell me something."

"All right," she agreed. "I'll stay right here and I'll call you if I hear anything."

He grasped her hands in his own, giving them a firm squeeze. "Thank you."

She watched him leave, then closed the door, waiting until she was completely alone to fall apart.

"I BLEW IT."

Harlan didn't seem surprised by his foster son's sudden appearance in his library or by his words. He closed the book in his lap and set it on the small table beside him.

"Have a seat, Nate."

Nate took the chair opposite Harlan, asking himself what he was doing here. His first inclination upon leaving Mia's house had been to find the nearest bar and get rip-roaring drunk. But he'd seen his mother fall into that pattern too many times, so instead he'd headed for the Longo estate, the scene with Mia playing over and over in his mind.

"She knows the truth?" Harlan guessed.

He gave a brisk nod. "Every sordid detail."

"I can tell by your face she didn't take it well. Maybe she just needs some time to let it sink in."

Nate stood up, too agitated to remain seated. He paced the Persian rug in front of the hearth, thinking of ways he could have handled it differently. But nothing would have blunted the truth. He'd seen the shock of his betrayal in her beautiful brown eyes.

"I doubt Mia will ever forgive me," Nate told him.

Harlan's brow crinkled. "Mia?"

Nate turned to face him, remembering too late that he didn't know about her masquerade. "That woman isn't Carleen Wimmer. It's her boss, Mia Maldonado."

Harlan's mouth twitched. "Really?"

"Yes, really." Nate resumed his pacing once more. "Some private investigator I turned out to be. I didn't even know I was chasing the wrong woman!"

"So now what happens?"

"Well, she won't be back tonight," Nate replied, avoiding the real question. "Or any other night. She never wants to see me again."

"I'm not concerned about the study," Harlan told him. "There are always unexpected developments in these kinds of experiments. Besides, there were only a few days left. We can still use most of the data."

"Why don't you just say it?" Nate challenged.

Harlan feigned innocence. "Say what?"

"I told you so." Nate stopped in front of the fireplace, gripping the oak mantle with one hand. "You warned me about lying to her. I should have seen this coming a mile away."

"Sometimes we only see what we want to see."

"And then we get blindsided."

Harlan settled back in his chair and crossed his legs. "You still haven't answered my question. What happens next?"

"Nothing happens." Nate stared into the flames. "I put it behind me. I forget I ever met Mia Maldonado."

"You sound so convincing," Harlan mused. "I almost believe you."

Nate met his gaze. "What other options are there? She kicked me out of her house—out of her life. The only choice I have is to survive."

"Like you did when your mother kicked you out of her life?"

Nate turned away from the fireplace. "I don't want to talk about her."

"I know," Harlan replied. "Yet, you keep repeating the same mistakes in your life. And I think they all go back to her."

Nate was in no mood to hear about all the times he'd messed up. "I didn't come here for a damn lecture."

"Well, that's too bad." Harlan rose to his feet. "Because you need to hear this before you screw up your life again."

"Hear what?" Nate challenged. "That I ruin every relationship I've ever had. I already know that."

Harlan shook his head. "You don't ruin them. You just bail out when it starts to get rough. Your mother had too many of her own problems to help you. The woman died of cirrhosis of the liver three years after giving you up. She probably thought that signing that parental release form would give you a better shot in life."

Nate shook his head. "Don't make her sound so noble. More likely she didn't think I was worth the trouble."

"She was a very sick woman, Nate. You can't let her rejection of you color every relationship you have for the rest of your life. Yes, you might lose Mia. I admit that's a real possibility."

"Very real," he agreed, remembering the look on her face.

"But you're not thirteen years old anymore. You're not a helpless little boy. You're a man. So if you love her, why don't you act like a man and fight for her?"

Anger, at himself and at the world, roiled inside of him. "I already asked Mia for a second chance. She didn't take me up on it."

"Because she was probably still too upset even to consider it. You have to give her some time to examine her heart."

"It's too late."

"Only if you decide to give up." Harlan looked like he wanted to shake him. "So you made a mistake. No relationship is perfect. Stop running away, Nate. Because you only end up running in circles."

As much as he hated to admit it, he couldn't deny the truth of Harlan's words. Nate had always fled relationships at the first sign of trouble, preferring to be the first one to leave.

Except with Mia. But it had been hard enough losing her once. He didn't think he could endure it again and keep his pride intact. "And if I fail?"

Harlan gave him a bittersweet smile. "Then you'll

be no worse off than you are at this moment." He leaned closer. "But what if you succeed?"

For the first time, Nate considered that possibility, almost hating the spark of hope it ignited deep inside of him. "I don't even know where to start."

"How about simply telling her how much you love her?" Harlan suggested.

That almost seemed too easy. "There's one problem with that plan. I don't think she'll see me or talk to me."

A voice sounded from the open doorway. "Maybe I can help you."

He turned and his jaw sagged when he saw the woman standing there. "What are you doing here?"

Carleen Wimmer lifted her chin. "If you promise not to give up on Mia, I'll tell you."

"I'm not giving up on her," Nate vowed.

"Then sit down," Carleen said, moving into the room. "Because it's a long story."

16

Mia sat alone in her living room as the hours slowly dragged by, waiting for word from Toby. It gave her too much time to think. Too much time for regret.

She pulled the folder Ian had given her out of the trash and carefully reviewed all the information inside. The documents showed Nate as a troubled youth, abandoned by his mother and eventually thrown into the foster care system. Despite her anger at his lies, she couldn't help the compassion that welled inside her as she learned some of the details about his past.

She'd been shocked by his deception. Hurt by his lies. But deep down inside, she knew that Nate wasn't responsible for Carleen's disappearance. He'd genuinely been as surprised as Mia when he'd seen the state of Carleen's room.

But he'd acted unhappy about it. Certainly not like a man satisfied with a job well done. Just as he hadn't reacted in anger when she'd revealed herself as Mia and not Carleen. In fact, once the initial surprise had worn off, he'd been relieved. His words rang in her head: *I'm just damn happy you're not engaged.*

Why would he care if he'd been playing her?

Mia rose from the sofa and walked to the window, looking out at the late afternoon shadows. There were still so many holes in the story, so many things she didn't understand. Had Carleen really been using an alias? And if so, why had her best friend been lying to Mia about her identity for over a year?

Too many questions without answers. But one thing she did know for sure. She still loved Nate—in spite of everything.

A car pulled into the driveway and Mia groaned when she saw the man behind the wheel. Sam Kowalski. No doubt he was here for the plans for his game room. She didn't want to deal with him and for a brief moment considered not answering the door.

But that was hardly professional. So she hurried over to the desk, digging through the drawer she'd just rearranged looking for the preliminary sketches she'd drawn up for him.

The doorbell rang before she could locate them.

"Sorry to bother you so late," Mr. Kowalski said, when she opened the door. "We're running behind at the plant, so I had to work longer than expected tonight."

"Not a problem," she replied, moving back to the desk. "I'll give you the plans I've drawn up and you can take them home and look them over. Perhaps we can set up an appointment next week to finalize the job."

He took a seat on the sofa. "Oh, it won't take me that long to decide. Once I make a decision about what's the right choice, I stick with it. The guys down at the plant even call me Bull because I'm so bull-headed about doing things right."

Mia finally located the file and pulled it out. "This really isn't a good time for me—"

"Just let me take a quick look," he interjected, reaching for the file.

She handed to him, but remained standing. "As you can see, I incorporated all of the elements we talked about earlier."

Mr. Kowalski frowned down at the plan. "What's this here?"

She leaned over for a better look. "That's a ceiling fan. For a room as large as your basement, I think you'll appreciate the circulation."

"How much does one of those cost?"

She swallowed a sigh of frustration. If he questioned her about every facet in the design plan, they'd be here all night. "It varies. They can run anywhere from fifty dollars to five hundred dollars."

He leaned back against the sofa, making himself comfortable. "Wow, that's quite a range. What's the difference between the fifty-dollar model and the five-hundred-dollar model?"

The phone rang and Mia almost leapt for joy at the interruption. She didn't care if it was one of those annoying telemarketers. She was going use it as an excuse to get rid of Mr. Kowalski.

"Excuse me a moment," she said, walking over to the desk as the phone rang a second time. She picked up the cordless receiver. "Hello?"

"Mia, it's me."

The sound of her friend's voice made her forget all

about her client. "Carleen? Oh, I'm so glad you called. Are you all right?" she demanded anxiously.

"Yes, I'm fine. I'm sorry if I worried you."

"What happened?" Mia asked. "Why did you disappear like that?"

"I'll tell you everything, but not over the phone. I'm at the Longo estate. Can you meet me here?"

She blinked in surprise. "What are you doing there?"

"I'll explain everything when you get here. Can you leave right now?"

Mia looked at Mr. Kowalski, who was still poring over the plan in front of him. "Absolutely. I'm on my way."

"See you soon," Carleen said, before disconnecting the line.

Mia set down the phone on the desk. "I'm so sorry, but I have an urgent appointment."

"No problem," he said, closing the folder and then rising to his feet with a grunt of exertion.

"I'll be happy to schedule an appointment with you sometime next week."

"That won't be necessary." He handed her the folder. "You've arranged it all perfectly."

His compliment surprised her. "I'm glad you're satisfied."

"Oh, I'm very satisfied." He reached into his coat pocket and pulled out a small revolver. "Now if you take me to my wife, I'll be ecstatic."

She stared at the gun pointed at her chest. "I don't understand."

"It's very simple really. I've been looking for my

beloved Angie for over a year—although I believe you know her as Carleen."

A chill shot through her at his words. "You don't want to do this, Mr. Kowalski."

"The name is Ray Perry," he sneered. "My wife isn't the only one who can play name games. But this crap has gone on long enough."

Mia didn't want to believe her best friend could ever have gotten involved with a man like this. "Carleen was married to you?"

He smiled coldly at her. "Till death do us part. At least, that's my way of thinking. Now, enough stalling. Let's go."

When Mia hesitated, Kowalski moved behind her, sticking the barrel of the gun into her spine. "Move it, lady."

She stood her ground, her knees shaking. "I won't let you hurt Carleen."

"Her name's Angie," he bit out. Then he leaned close behind her, his voice a harsh whisper in her ear. "The way I see it, you've been hiding my wife from me. So I might actually enjoy putting a bullet in your back. You might want to think about that before you do something stupid."

Mia needed to buy some time and that meant pretending to go along with him. She moved toward the door, her legs as heavy as lead. "All right. I'll take you to her."

The man grunted his approval and as they moved out into the fading twilight, Mia knew she had to think quickly. But she really had no choice.

She had to take him to Carleen.

"So that's my story," Carleen concluded with a sigh.

She and Nate sat alone in the library, the fire crackling in the hearth. Harlan had left them alone so he could watch for Mia's arrival, having already heard Carleen's story the night before when she'd come to the lab looking for Mia. That's when he'd offered her sanctuary.

Nate marveled at the way Carleen spoke so calmly about her past, though he could see her hands trembling slightly in her lap. She had married at the age of sixteen, finding out too late that her husband was both abusive and a control freak. She'd finally divorced him, even seeking a protection order, but his endless harassment and threats had never stopped.

The night Ray Perry had followed through on one of those threats, almost strangling her to death, was the night she'd left the small town of Claymore, Ohio, and her life as Angie Perry behind her.

"So you actually did reinvent yourself," Nate said. "New name. New life. New identity."

"I had no other choice," Carleen replied. "I had no family to help me and no money to fight him. As a former country commissioner, Ray knows the law well—at least well enough to evade any of the charges I tried to bring against him."

"And now you think he's found you."

"I'm sure of it," she said, the color leaving her face. "I know there's a fine line between paranoia and reality. So when we started receiving hang-up calls at the house, I told myself someone had just dialed a wrong number or was pulling a harmless series of pranks."

"You didn't want to believe it might be your ex-husband."

She shook her head. "Not after I'd worked so hard to make a new life for myself."

"But you never told Mia the truth?"

Anguish shone in her eyes. "I couldn't tell anyone. To protect them as much as myself. In order to survive, I had to become Carleen Wimmer. Angie Perry couldn't exist. Maybe it was selfish on my part, but I simply couldn't risk it."

"So Toby doesn't know anything about your past, either?"

She buried her head in her hands. "That's why I've been so crazy these last few weeks. I love Toby so much. Lying to him has torn me apart. But he's the only chance I might ever have of true happiness. I just wasn't strong enough to walk away."

Nate understood her dilemma. The Hamilton name offered power and security. She'd finally be safe from Ray Perry. He'd been in the same position once—alone and scared, with no place to go. Desperation can lead people in strange directions. He'd just been fortunate that it had led him to Harlan and Adele Longo all those years ago.

He glanced at his watch, anxious for Mia to arrive. She had a lot to digest today—not only Nate's duplicity, but Carleen's as well. At least Carleen had acted out of a need to survive. Nate couldn't claim such noble intentions. But he was determined to make it up to her somehow.

Because Mia Maldonado was the love of his life.

"I'm leaving tonight," Carleen announced. "After I tell Mia the truth—and Toby." Her lower lip quivered. "I owe them that much."

"Where will you go?"

She shrugged, uncaring. "Somewhere far away, to start over again. Harlan promised to help me. I don't know how I'll ever repay him."

"Worry about that later," Nate replied. "But I saw Toby tonight. I'm not so sure he'll be willing to let you go."

A lone tear spilled onto her cheek. "I can't drag him into this now. It's too dangerous. Ray found me. I didn't want to believe it at first. But too many things began to add up. The anonymous roses. That day I thought I saw him in the furniture store."

"So that's the real reason you abandoned us there."

She nodded. "I panicked. I ran for my car, then raced out of the parking lot, ready to leave Philadelphia and all my belongings behind. But the longer I drove, the more I began to doubt what I'd seen. I'd only glimpsed him for a moment. I managed to convince myself that it had been someone who just looked like Ray. Because I was certain that if it had been my ex-husband, he never would have let me go like that."

"So you came back to the house."

"Yes, I came back." She pulled a tissue out of her pocket and wiped her nose. "I thought if I could just hold on until Toby returned from Germany, we could be married and somehow everything would be all right. Now I know that was just a fantasy."

"You still haven't told me what scared you into running away last night."

"I knew he'd found me," she said, her voice almost a whisper. "I began to suspect it a week ago, when Mia told me about our newest client. A man who collects beer cans."

"I take it Ray collected beer cans."

"Yes. But I kept telling myself that was just a coincidence." She took a deep breath. "Then I found something that he'd given Mia. Something I hadn't really looked at closely until I'd started doing the books last night after Mia left for the sleep lab."

"What was it?"

"His check for the retainer to design a game room." She met his gaze. "He'd written our wedding date on the memo line. That's when I knew for certain that my life as Carleen Wimmer was over."

"It's not over," Nate assured her, his gut clenching at the fear he saw in her eyes. The fact that Mia had been so close to danger bothered him even more. "You have friends to protect you. Mia. Toby. Harlan and I. We won't let him hurt you again."

Carleen started to say something, but the words died on her lips when Harlan burst into the room.

"We've got a problem."

Nate had never seen his foster father so worked up before. "What is it?"

"Mia's just come through the front gate, but she isn't alone. There's a man with her." Harlan turned to Carleen. "You need to tell us if it's your ex-husband."

A low moan sounded in her throat, but she followed Harlan and Nate down the hallway to view the security videos. A camera tracked Mia on foot just past the gate, walking slightly ahead of the burly man behind her.

One look at Carleen's face told Nate what he didn't want to know.

"Oh, God," she breathed. "It's him."

Nate turned to Harlan, raw fear twisting inside of him. "He's got Mia."

Harlan nodded. "I know—and I doubt she'd bring him here voluntarily. Which means we have to prepare for the possibility that he's armed."

Nate turned back to the screen, watching Mia stumble, then fall to the ground. She got up slowly, rubbing her ankle.

"She's trying to slow him down until we spot them," he concluded. "She knows about the security cameras. I told her they covered the entire grounds."

"I've got to go out there," Carleen exclaimed, moving toward the door. "It's me he wants, not Mia."

Nate pulled her back. "No, you're not going anywhere."

"Don't you understand?" she cried. "He could hurt Mia. He'll do anything to get what he wants." She sagged against the wall in defeat. "That's why he always wins."

"He won't win this time," Nate vowed. "Not if I have anything to say about it."

Mia limped along the lawn, feigning a twisted ankle. Her heart beat painfully against her ribs and she hoped that somehow Carleen would see Ray on the security camera and make a run for it.

"Move, damn you," Ray said, pushing her forward.

She stumbled and fell to her knees. He yanked her up by her arm. "Stop stalling!"

Mia barely refrained from kicking him in the groin. The momentary satisfaction she'd feel would certainly not be worth getting shot. If violence wasn't the answer, maybe she could talk her way out of this situation.

"This really isn't the best way to win back Carleen," she began.

"I told you before, her name is Angie."

"Right. I keep forgetting." As they moved closer to the estate, her gaze scanned the multitude of windows, hoping Carleen was looking out of one of them.

"And I don't have to win her—she already belongs to me."

"Then why did she leave you?"

"Why do you ask so many nosy questions?"

Mia shrugged. "I'm just trying to understand."

"It's simple," he spat out. "Angie got confused. She convinced herself that she didn't want to be married to me anymore. But she's still my wife. That's not going to change."

Mia had no doubt that Carleen's confusion had ended the day she'd seen through this monster. He was a conceited blowhard who seemed to enjoy pushing women around. She just wished Carleen— or rather, Angie—had trusted Mia enough to tell the truth about her past.

This man eerily reminded her of Ian. Self-absorbed, concerned only with what he wanted. Treating woman like property. Ian had never hurt her—not physically. But how close had she come to facing the same fate as Carleen? What if she'd married Ian? Had children with him? What if he had become the kind of monster who held her captive now?

She suppressed a shiver at the close call.

"What kind of nut lives in a place this far from the road?" Ray said, his breathing heavier now.

"Dr. Longo is a scientist." Mia wanted to keep him talking. The more she communicated with him, the less likely he was to shoot her. At least, that's what she remembered hearing on some television special about kidnapping years ago. But she'd never actually imagined herself as a hostage.

"He conducts sleep studies in a lab he designed himself," she continued. "It's a little unorthodox, but he's a very nice man."

"So how does he know Angie?" Ray asked, kicking a chicken out of his path.

"She signed up for one of his sleep studies." Mia didn't bother to mention that she'd gone in Carleen's place.

Ray snorted. "She probably has trouble sleeping without me beside her."

Mia sincerely doubted that was the case. The man had a serious inability to let go. Much like Ian.

The one man who didn't seem to have a problem letting her go was Nate. Her heart twisted when she remembered some of the words she'd said to him. Words spoken out of fear that he didn't really love her. Now she might never see him again. Never have a chance to discover if their relationship was real. To tell him that she loved him.

And she wanted that chance.

As they neared the estate, a door swung open and Carleen stepped outside. Mia opened her mouth to shout a warning, but Ray slapped his hand over her lips, smothering her words.

They stood there in silence, half hidden behind the school bus, watching Carleen walk leisurely toward the sleep lab.

Mia squirmed in his grasp, but Ray held her tight until Carleen went through the door of the sleep lab.

"Gotcha," Ray said under his breath. Then he pushed Mia aside and ran in pursuit of his wife.

17

MIA SCRAMBLED UP from the lawn and gave chase, but Ray had gotten too much of a head start. He reached the sleep lab first, bursting through the door and leaving it open behind him.

She followed right on his heels, gasping for breath when she finally reached the doorway, too winded to give warning to all the research subjects and lab assistants inside.

But to her surprise, Harlan was the only person in sight. He stood inside the hub, directly in front of the central control panel.

His eyes widened at their arrival. "What's going on here?" he asked, looking back and forth between the two of them.

Ray waved his gun, motioning Mia into the lab. "Go stand by the old man."

She had no choice but to follow his instructions, her mind racing. Why had Carleen even gone into the sleep lab? And where was she now?

Ray had the same question. "Where is she?"

"Excuse me?" Harlan said.

His eyes narrowed. "You heard me. I'm looking for my wife. You probably call her Carleen."

"Now listen here," Harlan began, stepping protectively in front of Mia. "There's no need to be swinging that gun around. If you just put it away, perhaps we can talk about this rationally."

"I don't want to make trouble for you," Ray replied, ignoring Harlan's suggestion. "I just want my wife."

Mia saw Harlan glance reluctantly toward the Elvis suite. Ray followed his gaze and then smiled. "She's in there?"

"Don't hurt her," Harlan implored.

"I don't want to hurt anybody," Ray replied, his gun still trained on them as he moved toward the suite. "I just want to get my wife so we can be on our way. We have a lot of catching up to do."

"No," Mia cried, taking a step toward him.

But Harlan grabbed her and whispered, "It'll be all right."

She didn't see how—but something told her to trust him.

Ray nodded his approval at their acquiescence. "Just stay where you are and nobody will get hurt."

Then he disappeared inside the Elvis suite.

A moment later, Mia heard the crack of bone, followed by a yowl of pain. The door opened and Nate stepped into the hub, rubbing his knuckles.

"Are you crazy?" Mia yelled at him, catching sight of an unconscious Ray lying on the floor, his nose swelling. "He had a gun."

Nate grasped her by the shoulders. "He had you! I wasn't about to let him hurt you—or take Carleen."

Mia turned to Harlan. "You knew about this."

"My son has a wicked one-two punch. I'm sure Ray never even saw it coming."

"What about Carleen?" Mia asked, her heart still racing.

"I'm right here." Carleen stood in the doorway of another suite.

Relief flooded through her. "I was so worried about you."

Carleen ran over and hugged her. "I could say the same about you! Are you all right?"

"I'm fine," Mia assured her. "But I'm still a little confused about what just happened here."

"We saw you on the security camera," Carleen explained, "and decided to set a trap. It was all Nate's idea."

"The police are on their way," Harlan informed her. "I called them right before we set the plan in motion."

Mia started shaking, a delayed reaction from everything that had just transpired. She reached for a chair, grabbing it before her legs gave out from under her. Nate knelt down beside her, taking her hand in his.

"I'm sorry," he said.

She didn't know whether to strangle him or kiss him. "You should be. Don't ever put your life in danger like that again."

A smile kicked up one corner of his mouth. "No, I mean I'm sorry for deceiving you, Mia. I'll spend the rest of my life trying to make it up to you."

Before she could reply, the outer door to the sleep lab opened and Mia turned to see Toby walk inside. He made a beeline for Carleen, pulling her into his arms.

"Thank God you're all right," he cried. "I was at the police station when the call came in. I've never been so scared in my life."

Carleen blanched. "What did you hear?"

"That your abusive ex-husband was after you," Toby replied, still holding her. "That he had Mia at gunpoint while he searched for you."

"I'm so sorry I never told you about Ray," Carleen said, a thick sob in her throat. "It wasn't fair to you, I know. But I was so afraid I'd lose you if you knew the truth."

Toby looked intently into her face, his hands on her shoulders. "You'll never lose me," he vowed. "We're getting married."

"But your mother…" Carleen began.

He leaned down to kiss her. "My mother is out of my life—at least until she learns to accept the choices I make. That includes accepting the woman I love. If she disowns me, so be it. Maybe it's time I learned to stand on my own two feet."

The police swarmed into the sleep lab, weapons drawn. But Ray was no longer a threat to them or anyone else. He'd suffered a broken nose and a cracked jaw, courtesy of a former juvenile delinquent who had stolen Mia's heart.

The police dragged Ray out of the sleep lab, and then the lead officer waved Harlan over and began conferring with him.

Carleen wiped the tears off her cheeks. "I can't believe this nightmare is finally over."

"You won't have to live in fear anymore," Toby said, circling his arm around her waist. "Your jerk of an ex-husband will be prosecuted for kidnapping, at the very least. He'll be going away for a very long time."

Harlan returned to confirm Toby's prediction. "The police will be charging Mr. Perry with so many felonies that he'll never bother any of you again. They need to take our statements, though. Carleen and Toby, why don't you come with me to the library? The detective will join us there soon."

That left her alone in the sleep lab with Nate.

"Are you really all right?" she asked, looking at his bruised knuckles.

"No," he replied solemnly. "I haven't been all right since you kicked me out of your house. Not that I blame you. I should have told you the truth about my job with Beatrice Hamilton long before you found out about it."

"You're not the only one who lied," Mia reminded him. "But the truth is that I haven't had the best relationships with men in my life. So when I discovered you weren't really interested in me, I was hurt."

"I *was* interested in you," Nate countered. "Much too interested to do the job I was supposed to do. And you don't know how damn glad I am that you're not the one engaged to Hamilton."

"Me, too," she agreed. "I couldn't stand it if…"

"If?" he prodded.

She swallowed, ready to lay her heart on the line. "If you didn't really love me."

"I'm not going to tell you that I love you."

Her heart twisted at his words, but before she could react, he walked over and took her by the hand. "I'm going to prove it to you."

Mia let Nate lead her into the Elvis suite, wondering what exactly he had in mind. He sat her on the edge of the bed, but instead of joining her there, he turned to the jukebox.

She watched while he extracted the electrode leads from the jukebox. Without saying a word, he attached them one by one to his temples and forehead. When he was completely hooked up, he knelt down beside her.

She had to bite back a smile at the picture he presented.

"You think this is funny?" he asked, amusement dancing in his eyes.

"You do look a little ridiculous," she admitted. "Cute, but ridiculous. What in the world are you doing?"

"I'm proving, by strictly scientific means, just how much I love you." He leaned closer. "Now kiss me."

Her doubts about his love melting away, she bent down to give him a chaste kiss on the cheek.

He arched a brow. "You call that a kiss?"

"Maybe I can do better," she said playfully. Then she circled her arms around his neck and pulled him to her, the momentum catapulting both of them back onto the bed.

She kissed him full on the lips, pouring everything she had into it. Her heart. Her soul. Her unconditional love. Her initial hypothesis about Nate hadn't held up. He wasn't Mr. Wrong. He was absolutely right for her.

A deep moan rumbled in his chest as he kissed her back. Their bodies arched toward each other as their mouths melded together. He rolled on top of her, the electrode wires hanging from his head tickling her nose and chin.

He leaned up on his elbows, staring down at her with a satisfied smile on his face. "Now I have you exactly where I want you."

She arched a brow. "So what are you going to do about it?"

"Wait right here," he demanded, then tore off the electrodes attached to his head before disappearing out the door.

Before she even had time to miss him, he returned carrying a scroll of paper in his hands.

Mia sat up as he joined her on the bed. "What is that?"

"It's my scientific proof." He carefully unfurled the printout from the biomonitor. Then he pointed to the top line. "This is the heart rate line—see how much it's elevated? Here are the skin sensors—also elevated. Breathing rate is accelerated substantially. Which means I'm either having a heart attack or I'm in love."

"Should I take that as a compliment?"

He smiled, drawing her into his arms. "Definitely. I love you, Mia Maldonado, beyond a scientific doubt."

"And I love you, Nate Cafferty." She tossed the paper aside, then reached out and began unbuttoning his shirt. "Which I intend to prove the old-fashioned way."

"I like the sound of that," he replied, as her hands spread his shirt open. "By the way, I found a bed for my room."

"Where?" she asked, hoping he hadn't gone shopping at the Furniture Warehouse again.

"Right here," he said, patting the mattress beneath them. "It has a lot of sentimental value, so Harlan offered to sell it to me. He'll even throw in the jukebox. If my decorator approves."

"I definitely approve," she said, sliding his shirt over his broad shoulders. "It's the perfect bed."

"No, not perfect." He caught her hands in his own, then gazed into her eyes. "Not unless you're in it."

Her heart leapt but she remained silent.

"I'd like us to try a little experiment of our own—to prove my hypothesis that sleeping with a stranger can lead two people to live happily ever after."

Mia blinked back tears of joy. "And when do you intend to test this hypothesis?"

He smiled, pulling her down on the bed with him as Elvis began to serenade them. "Every night, for the rest of our lives."

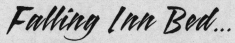

If you enjoyed what you just read,
then we've got an offer you can't resist!

Take 2 bestselling
love stories FREE!

Plus get a FREE surprise gift!